Cautionary Tales
for Serious Seekers of Truth

About the Writer

Charley Lane lives in Australia with her partner and a very good dog. They like to wonder about the world and the universe and go on exploring adventures.

Charley writes tales about millennia past, present, and future for people aged 12 and onward to learn from, so they can grow in wisdom and navigate a more wonderful life through a better understanding of themselves, their uniqueness, their choices, and the intricate world and universe they live in, and the power of truth that exists.

She writes in the early morning when everyone is asleep, for it is then that the light and wisdom comes and each tale is brought to life.

The helper who writes

Charley Lane

Cautionary Tales
for Serious Seekers of Truth

Olympia Publishers
London

www.olympiapublishers.com
OLYMPIA PAPERBACK EDITION

Copyright © Charley Lane 2024

The right of Charley Lane to be identified as author of
this work has been asserted in accordance with sections 77 and 78 of
the Copyright, Designs and Patents Act 1988.

All Rights Reserved

No reproduction, copy or transmission of this publication
may be made without written permission.
No paragraph of this publication may be reproduced,
copied or transmitted save with the written permission of the publisher,
or in accordance with the provisions
of the Copyright Act 1956 (as amended).

Any person who commits any unauthorised act in relation to
this publication may be liable to criminal
prosecution and civil claims for damage.

A CIP catalogue record for this title is
available from the British Library.

ISBN: 978-1-80439-210-2

This is a work of fiction.
Names, characters, places, and incidents originate from the writer's
imagination. Any resemblance to actual persons, living or dead, is
purely coincidental.

First Published in 2024

Olympia Publishers
Tallis House
2 Tallis Street
London
EC4Y 0AB

Printed in Great Britain

Dedication

To those who have supported me in the toughest of times, I love and thank you.

From my soul to yours,

Charley

Foreword

Called to write for the hope of this world, the poorness of the writer is absolved and the richness of the author revealed—the author with a name not written here or spoken of without awe.

Be that as it may, the writer does have a name: Charley Lane—and her real name to keep for herself to own. And this is the reason why her real name must never be known: a secret of sorts to help her be at peace without interruption from those who want history retold in their own way—the way of the world without a power to care for it…

A power seen by some but not by others, called by many but written by few, and the true author of these tales of truth arranged for this generation; a light to live by.

Sincerely yours,
A close friend.

Preface

I am a small person with a big view of this world and the next; always I have looked and learned, and always I have sought.

The seeker of truth is the one who finds it, and though it may take a long time, it is there. And I have shared the truths I have found in this book—for this is my book: the book of the helper who writes.

Charley Lane
charleylane.com

Introduction

The trials of humans and the world they live in are such that no one has every answer. There is a power that rules though, and it has the answers—and that power is truth.

This edition has many truths, and there are many more to be shared. If this day you wish to have these truths, all you need to do is read and learn from the power who wrote them, as the power who wrote them has this to say to you right now: "Forever, this world needs my wisdom, and forever it needs my words."

Read them and know, this day, your wishes for truth have come true. Time therefore to begin…

CHAPTER ONE

SELF AND CHOICES

THE PLACE OF BELONGING

Kindness was in the heart of the young boy who went to the city. He knew in his heart he was going to be a better person for going there, so he went to see if he could make his fortune.

The day wore on, and still he had found no rest or any help from another person. He went from house to house to ask for help, but no one saw him; he was ignored.

He had left the home of his parents to find his fortune, but no fortune found him; instead, he was left alone, with the kindnesses from his home gone and never returning.

He saw all the people walking in the city and looking happy. He saw the many homes that were so beautiful; he could not understand how they could be that way? He saw lovely presents under the trees and wondered why he had none? And he called to other boys of his age, yet they ignored him—he only wanted to be their friend.

The day of his leaving home was the day of his poorness, and he regretted it for, had he stayed, his bed was safe, his food was safe, and his kindness was safe. But there, he had no money to spend for himself, so he thought the wonder of the city could help him—if he could just find a job. After all, the city has lights, the city has jobs, and the city has lots of friends and people who care. 'And they will surely help me,' he thought.

However, the city has no friends, and the lights are switched off at night, and then he is alone in the darkness without a friend, or help, or any money to buy food. In this way, he calls himself poor, but he was wealthy at home in the country. The country has less jobs and less lights, but the people are like they should be—always kind, always giving, and always a friend is there when a friend is needed.

The boy considered his challenges at the home of his parents and his challenges in the city of beautiful homes and people who call themselves friends to all yet do not see him, and given time, he came to his senses, saying to himself, "I will call my mother and ask if it is all right for me to return to her home of my childhood."

On hearing his voice, his mother leapt for happiness, for her son had remembered her and remembered her kindness and her love! And her son is saying he wants to return to the place of his birth—a place that has comfort and homeliness and belonging.

And, in belonging, the boy, saddened by his lack of faith in his home, remembers the city as a place of even greater sadness, for his friends in the country knew him enough to call on his name and visit, but no one in the city was a friend. Not really. Not ever. Instead, they call themselves friends to others, yet do not believe it enough to work for it.

This day, if you see a boy who needs a home, reach out and touch his hand, for his is the hand of friendship forever.

YOU WILL SEE

"So," asked the man to himself, "where am I now that I have so much in my home and life and can look back on it?" Seeing his image in a photo, he wondered who the young person was: 'I cannot remember this man inside, or what he thought, or how he viewed this world of blue and green and pink and yellow. Who was I then, when the man I am now is the man I wanted to be?'

The man in the photo considered this question and raised his eyes to see himself in the future. "Who are you?" he said to the man he called himself. "I think you are someone who has been untrue to yourself and who has been called into the world I despise so much and made into itself."

"Not so," answered the lighter man than he had been. "I considered all my dealings with the world and made choices along a journey that gave me greater understandings than you have this day. Now do you see? I was not right in how I thought about many things, and now I am in wonder at this and see someone I do not know."

"I do not understand," said the young man, who looked puzzled and hurt all at once. "You are me, and I am you. Where did I go that I am you?"

"You went to lands and workplaces and relationships, and British outcomes for politics. You saw the truth and were told lies. You knew others who liked you and some who did not. You made friends and enemies and gave yourself hardships and disasters. You lied and told some people you were angry, and you made friends disappear—and lovers too.

"You grew in like-mindedness with the light and air and soil. You learned about yourself and your favourite things, and not some, but others, hurt you. You lived and dreamed and failed and rose again from the ashes and saw great wonders in the process.

"You liked some people who wanted to be friends but were not in the end. You made greater friends over long times together—in touch and in friendship with each other. You learned that you are not perfect and are often right and often wrong. Your soul survivor won, and your gritted aspirations also. You tried and failed, and you tried and succeeded.

"You are myself without any of these wrested attributes and wonders. You are youth, and youth is unsure of who they actually are until their working life is visible, when in fact, it is not work but family and friends and thoughts thought and left unthought that make a man or child into an adult.

"You are me; it is said and known, and I am you, but we do not think the same—not yet anyway—but you will, for life has a way of helping each person grow in times of trouble and rest in times of none. You will see."

"I did."

TWO PLACED TOGETHER

The marriage was to be on Saturday. It had much to do for the parents of the bride and the parents of the groom, who thought, 'If my child marries their heaven-sent loved one, I will be so unbelievably happy, for this is a marriage made in heaven!'

The day came, and all in the party were excited at being part of the day and the marriage of the bride and the groom they cared so much for. A matter had come to their attention, though, and this was their concern: 'Had the man betrayed his wife-to-be?' A person had said he had, and now all were concerned.

"Was this the truth?" they asked themselves and their close confidants.

The chosen man had no understanding of this and was merry in his preparations. He shaved his beard and touched his face, thinking, 'I am so happy! This is the day I am to be married to the most wonderful person I have ever met, and she loves me—I am so happy!' he thought to himself again over and over.

The time drew near to go to the church where the couple had

met on their first date, and soon it had grown into love—for they were young and very happy with each other. Just as the time arrived to hasten, a friend stopped by to tell the man what he had heard. The man was so amazed that he quickly stooped to the ground in heartfelt dismay.

"I have not been this way!" he exclaimed. "I have not done this thing to my beautiful wife and cannot bear to let this be announced to her!"

At this moment, a friend of the bride arrived.

"The marriage is off!" she said. "A matter has come to my friend's attention that you have been unfaithful, and she does not wish to join with you in life, for her life has been happy and is now lost in unhappiness. You have done this thing, and now it is you who must pay!"

The cheating accuser was this friend; she loved the man and was about to get her dream outcome, for she would comfort him in his agony and be there for him when he needed someone.

A cunning person who has no morals has no place in this man's life, as this man took his life that day. And the world that watched mourned, for they came to know his pain—he had not been a cheater; instead, he had been cheated upon.

To do these things is not right. Those that have been placed together must not be pulled apart, and those who plan this are in their own anger and distaste to others. Let this not be you. Trust in the world to be your friend, and it will be a friend to you.

Ask, and you too will find a true partner to love you.

EARNING IS BETTER

When someone has a nice area to live in, they are well thought of, and have people say to themselves, "They have a nice home, so they are rich and have more than we do."

And when someone has a nice car, people think to themselves, 'They have a nice car and are rich and have more than we do.'

And when someone has nice clothes, people think to themselves, 'They have nice clothes and are rich, and have more than we do.'

But when someone has a fool in their home who brings them down to a level below the house, the car, and the clothes, people are glad, for they know their own home is better than the one who has everything.

If this day your fool has brought you down to the level of those who think this way, do not concern yourself with the foolishness of the fool but, rather, with buying more things to make people know you have the things you have because you work for them, and they do not—for a fool is never as great a burden as one who does not work for a living.

Earning is better than sloth, and no one who earns will ever be brought undone by a fool. Causes and effect pardon those that suffer fools, but for those that suffer another's laziness, the cause is the effect.

THINK OF THEIR LOVE

The work of the old man had wrought much pain in his being—he had sore everything, and nothing was without pain. He was old and wanted to be young again, so he looked to the medical profession for help.

The doctors said, "You can have a facelift, and we can make your body strong again with these pills."

He took the pills and had the facelift, and his wonderful youth was back! His body changed, and he decided to find love again. He met a lady, and they fell in love and were joined to one another. He called her his wife, and she called him her husband, and they were happy.

After a time went by, the man thought he should meet someone else to see if he could be even happier. He looked at a lady, and they were joined. She seemed more exciting than the lady he was with, so he gave this lady his love, and they were in a relationship of sorts.

He did not tell his wife about this, as she was still pretty and loved him so much that he felt good about himself. But the other lady was someone he could be physical with and not care about whether he said things that were not what someone should say to a lady—and they had fun in places that should be inside, not outside.

Time passed, and the lady he called his wife became aware of this infatuation and was called into a place of such hurt that she considered leaving her partner. He was shocked and frightened, for he realised he loved her beauty inside and her beauty outside, and she meant much more to him than the one he had been a fool for!

He was frightened that he had wounded his wife so much that she would never forgive him. He was also frightened he would be alone without her love, which made him feel so wonderful inside. He was very sorry and asked for forgiveness and for her to love him again.

The woman looked inside her heart and knew men to not be all they should to their wives, for she herself had been a friend to a married man once and betrayed his wife many times. She knew this man she had for a friend had not been her husband and had loved her in her way—but not in the way of a wife—and now she was the wife. She knew she must forgive her man and let him make it up to her in ways he could in times of health and happiness, so she said, "I forgive you" and "I love you" to him, and he was made whole in an instant!

This day, if you have a man who wanders and is sorry, thank yourself for being his partner and being safe in your joint home, and live with the indiscretion—if this is what you choose—for if you do not, your home may fall, and your life may change for the worse.

And if you are a man considering being indiscreet with another, think of their love for you and your love for your wife, and look not upon their body as something to be caught in romance with, but on the body of your wife, who gave herself to you in love, not lust, and in joy, not discourse—for your romantic interest may be your downfall.

COINS

Roles are often made better when they are withheld from the role of the generous. Roles are made better because they own their many coins and few dollars.

However, the role of the generous does not make way for dollars but for coins.

The day people give their coins to those who need, is the day when those who need, need no more.

LOVE FORGOTTEN

Love was at home in the house, and the ones in love were good with it. Love had found them and made them happy in their lives, which were otherwise alone and without friendship—love was wonderful!

Time passed, and love became final, for the ones that loved forgot their love for one another and, instead, made their distaste known.

"Why are you like this?"
"Why do you do this?"
"Why do you not do this?"
"Why are you so unkind to me?"
"Why are you not like you used to be?"
"Why have you stopped loving me?"

Love had left the home of the pair and made them unhappy, for they said, "I loved the wrong person when I should have loved myself."

When this happens, love has no place left to go...

Today has been a wonderful day, for we were in love. Tomorrow is not so, for we forgot what love was and made it into hate, and hate has no love to give to another—all hate does is feed itself. And now self is alone.

BE GRATEFUL

One day, a lady went to have a bet and won! She loved the win and thought, 'I can do this more and will change my life this way—as it is easy!'

The days passed, and she won, and lost, and won, and lost, and won, and lost, and won, and lost. And she looked at herself and thought, 'I can do better. I will bring this lifestyle into my house and make it my living.'

Her calling was here at last! Work made her unhappy, and she wanted a way to live as she wanted to live and to be the person she wanted to be—a relaxed and happy person, not a harried and unhappy person, so this is what she did.

After a time, she went to a friend and said, "I have no money and need a job. Can you give this to me?"

The friend had a friend who had a job and could give it to her, so the friend said, "Yes, I can help this way."

The job was not nice, though, as the manager was harsh and said not-nice things to the lady, and she worked harder than before and earned less. And, in earning less, she realised that the job she gave away paid much more and was much easier than she had known it to be.

Today, she has this job again but has not remembered to come into it being grateful, for there are people who have terrible jobs and no money and no hope for more in life—and it is these people who need work to live and drink and eat plain meals and wish for jobs that have what the lady has.

For those who already have much and want more, remember this tale—for, in wanting more, you sometimes get less.

PLACED IN YOUR HANDS
One day, a man went to the country to buy a horse he thought could win races for him. The horse was perfect! It had good conformation and a nice pedigree, and the man thought, 'This horse will win many races.'

And it went well for a time, but after this time, people who shared the horse wanted more than the horse could give. The horse tried and tried but could give no more, and everyone thought the horse was unable to try more and sold it.

The man who thought the horse was better, bought it and made a wonderful life for himself, for his belief was greater than that of those who gave up easily—for giving up is not an option when you have committed to something placed in your hands by a power you know not where it comes from.

Adjust and succeed.

TRY AND SEE
The lady had a new job, and she was very happy as it was in a place she liked, and the people were very nice. The job was someone else's though, so it was only for a short time, but the

lady liked the job so much that she wished it was her own and made sure she was very good at it so people might believe it would be better that she had it.

While working, she did not know she was being watched by others who had better jobs for her—if she wanted them—for now, they could see how good she was at her work. And that her previous role was not one that suited her extraordinary abilities with computers and other things like making reports and dates for events and calling people with a smile.

The lady worked hard and didn't see the job opportunities posted internally and didn't apply for them; she did not think she could apply, as she was in a temporary role that needed a commitment met—for the lady she worked for was very nice to have given it to her.

Time passed, and the new job became busier as she was given more tasks and more responsibilities. The hours flew by, and soon the days and weeks and months passed, and now it was time to go back to her old job. This was devastating, as the lady did not like her old job, or the place it was located, or the people she worked with.

The soundness of her skills was there for all to see, but the soundness of her decision to be committed to one person who had helped her instead of applying for other jobs was not sound at all.

The day has many choices in it: the choice to be committed and the choice to be bettered by trying and seeing what happens. That day is today—do not wait for tomorrow, for tomorrow may be different from what you would have it be. Always seek.

THE ADVENTURES OF LIFE

One day, a small animal was walking and went to see if she could find something to smell and eat if it was nice. She walked a long way and went to a place she knew well, for her mother walked her there often, and it was safe and secure, and she knew her way home.

The small dog was happy; here was a smell, and there was a smell, and here was something to consider eating, and there was something to consider eating. Time passed, and she was enjoying herself so much—the day was much more exciting on a walk than being at home on the doorstep waiting for her mother to come!

Hours went by before a car arrived with someone who looked friendly and called to her.

The small dog looked at the person and thought, 'This is a good person who will be nice to me. I will see what they are like to be with for a while, then I will go home.'

The person patted the dog, and they made friends.

The person looked at the dog and thought, 'This dog is lost. I will care for the dog and take her with me and see if I can find her owner.'

Later that day, a friend called the owner to say the dog's picture was on the local news post, so the owner called a friend to ask her to collect her dog right away and take the puppy home.

That night, the owner scolded the dog and made it known she was not to stray, for it had given her a fear she might start to do it all the time.

The dog looked at her owner and thought, 'I was still at home, for my home has many miles, and they belong to me, and I would come home just when I was ready to end my adventure. I will go again, but this time, I will not make friends with a stranger in case they call me away with them and do not bring me home—for this was my concern."

A day is a large one for a beast that roams and a small one for a beast that does not. If your beast chooses to roam, take them outside more and let them see the day and smell the smells and know they are safe within their area, and live with the occasional adventure.

For the adventures of life are the moments when we are all free to enjoy that which the day brings to us. And the small aspects of the one who has much to give others are better than the large aspects of the ones who do not.

Listen, then, to your own callings for adventure and take yourself outside, for the day has much to give.

THE FUNDAMENTAL MEASURE

A kind person said to another kind person, "I wish you had a better life and will try to help you get it."

The person who had the life that was being bettered was attuned to this and answered, "Thank you so much. I would like that!" and together, they worked to make the friend's life better until, one day, it was.

The friend was so unsettled by the change in his circumstances that he fell from grace because he could not cope with the money and fortunes it gave to him.

The man was sorely sorry he had ever bettered his life and said to his friend, "I wish you had never helped me, as I was happy before and did not know I needed a better life, for now I am never going to find that way again."

Soon after, he died and went to heaven, where he found what he had been wanting all along. The days and years passed, and one day, his friend who had helped him also came to heaven. The friend had been a friend to many and had made himself a mansion in heaven where many came to bring their friendship and enjoy his house and make it wonderful.

The man was thoughtful about this and said to himself, "I should have been more thankful than I was, as I am here but never helped anyone like this friend has."

And so it was that he learned, at last, the fundamental measure of life in the world: the measure of help we give to others.

SELF-MADE

One day a boy went to the maker of his best friend's home and said, "Help me to make homes like this one, as I would like to build it myself."

The maker said to the boy, "I will let you help me for a time, but after that, you must be employed, as I cannot do this for you."

The boy agreed and helped the maker for a time. He then went to another maker and asked to do the same. The maker agreed, and the boy did the same.

After a time, the maker could no longer let the boy continue working without being paid and said to him, "You are someone who has a good heart and a good ethic for work. I will give you a job and teach you my trade, for my trade is a good one, as I have built my own life from it and have a wonderful way of living. My house is also a good house, and one that has much love and laughter in it—for we are very happy with our life."

The boy went to the maker's job and stayed there for some time, learning how to be just like his mentor.

The boy became a man and said to the maker, "I am now ready to make my own way in the world and see if I can be like you," so he went outside of the maker's job and made his own work.

The crafts he worked at made him a name, and he went from workplace to workplace being handsomely rewarded until, one day, he made his own house for his new wife and found the life he had worked so much for.

If this day you have no such life and no such hope in finding work, be like the boy. For in this way, you will succeed where others fail.

CHAPTER TWO

SEEK AND TRY

THE FIRST GIFT

The sun went over the hill, and night came. The night brought with it long magnitudes of sleep that those in the house enjoyed, for sleep is a calling to another world full of exciting tales and wonders—or full of dreadful things if your hope is without the one who can help at these times.

The night was one of wonders in the house, for all within it were guided by the one who helps, and all were at peace with their place in life.

Soon the morning broke and a new day dawned, bringing adventures that were made to be lived in and made for those that lived in the house of belief. A train arrived carrying friends and people to visit and make happiness in their company and in their workplaces and in their friendships with others.

The day slowly travelled across the sky, and everyone was tired at its end, deciding to rest and sleep again. The sleep renewed them, and, once more, they made the day their gift, and the gift of the day was given to them.

If this day you have no rest, no sleep, and no gifts to open in the day or night, think upon this story and seek to understand it; for in understanding, you will gain the first gift, and then the next, until your days are filled with greatness and blessings.

QUALIFICATIONS

"Finally, it's done!" said the small mouse clicker.

"Finally, it's done!" said the smaller mouse clicker.

Click, click, click, click, click—so forever they clicked, on and in and under and over, clicking their prices and making calculations.

One day the worker said, "I am over this smaller way of clicking and will see if I can get the giant wages I can command now that I have made the clicks end in a qualification," and on she went into the space race of job applying and made her mark in the City of Angels with wings that make clicks come true.

'I love this city,' thought the lady who had made her dream job appear. 'This city has given me a good wage, and now that I no longer need my part-time job, I can spend as much as I want on myself.'

And this is what she did: she spent and spent and spent until her spending became a new way of living. She had much in her wardrobe and much in her cupboards, and now she had much in her house of betterment—for her house was now a new home with wonderful things to look at and sit beside.

'My clicks were worth it, as now I am happier than I have ever been!' Or so she thought… for one day, the job she had was no more and the work she had was no more—for she had been superseded by another person who had ended their clicks with a degree in accounting. And the one who had the degree spent her money on clothes, and trips, and saucy things to wear at night—for her love of herself was great.

And so on went the cycle of buying and buying and buying until the time when the value of the qualifications went to the garbage—for garbage it was to the employers who wanted more and more and more from their staff. More highly paid, more highly qualified, and more highly sought-after workers were made into busy people making busy money for their owners—owners who cared not for them personally but for their attributes while they were useful.

And the cycle continued and went on into times of forever-made workers making forever-made calculations and forever-made profits that soared beyond that which was fair, or even possible—if profit was not so important that it cut people out of the diagonal of soared aspirations.

Too soon, the workers disappeared, and too soon, their jobs went elsewhere—to other countries and to computers and to people that weren't real people but robots of different kinds.

'Alas,' thought the lady who had clicked so much at the start, she had won her day.

'Alas,' thought the next who had done the same.

And a time passed where they went into retirement and made less money, and had less things to eat and drink, and less time for friends—because seeing friends costs money.

"Alas," said the friends, "our friends are alone with no one to see or help them. What shall we do…? We know—we will send some clicks!"

And that is the story: the story of clicks. Clicks for tomorrow are never clicks for the years ahead, only tomorrow. Make sure to keep clicking your money value upward, for the day you stop is the day you fail, and failure is the finalisation of the time of being free to spend all that which you enjoy.

Qualify yourself, and you will be free in this day and the next.

CHOOSE TO OVERCOME

The days were longer and longer, and still no one came. The man was unhappy that his own hands had caused his downfall, and now, no one wanted to be with him in the self-employed workplace he'd made after the day of his fall and job loss.

He looked at himself and wondered, 'What shall I do? Shall I be at peace with this time and make it my place of calling? Or should I be unhappy about what has happened and make this my place of calling?'

He wondered this often and said this to himself every day.

Time passed and work finally came. It was small at first, and then more and more came to ask for his help, as he had been a help to them before his fall and now, he could be of help again.

The man was much happier and remembered that he can choose to be unhappy or happy, and he decided to let others know this is a choice everyone has.

To be happy is to choose to overcome, and to be unhappy is to choose a fight you cannot ever win. This day, if you are not where you wish to be, choose to be happy, for no waiting time is ever called into being without there being a reason—a reason for making choices that change the days ahead. Fruition is made this way.

A FRIEND INDEED

Somewhere there is a human who has much to consider when making their own friends into enemies. Those who make friends into enemies should remember that, before they do this, they should be peaceful with the consequences, for enemies often become powerful in their revenge.

This day, if you are considering making a friend into an enemy, first consider whether you will be able to defend yourself if that wholly justified human decides to come against you—for those that make enemies are the enemy, and if you are the enemy, you cannot be a friend to others.

Keep the friends you have and make more, for otherwise, there will come a time when you have no friends to help you in your old age, and then you will be alone without help.

A friend in need is a friend indeed, and those who make

enemies have no friends. Start this way, and you will finish this way. Forever alone; a game over.

REAL FAME

The one thing the child wanted more than anything was to be famous and for everyone to see how special he was. He looked in the mirror and thought, 'No one is like me. I am very handsome and intelligent, and I have gifts no one knows of. I will be famous, and people will love me for who I am—because I am special!'

The man grew into his own body and soon saw himself in front of crowds of adoring fans on social media. He had many followers, and they said he was an influencer who could be followed because of his looks, intelligence, and gifts for being special.

Time passed, and the man started to worry that he had no money to keep up the pretences of his lifestyle. He looked to those who could help and found no one there—for there were others more exciting than him and better looking and with better lifestyles. And he started to be concerned that his fame was dwindling and wondered what he could do to be famous forever?

He decided that if he could not be famous in life, he would be famous in death, and he took his own life with people watching. That day, he went to heaven and found that his name was not in the book at the doorway and was turned away; he had failed to see in life that he could have meaning for others and not himself and that he could make the world a better place instead of placing himself at its centre.

A person without good works is a person who has nothing to show the gates that await, and forever is a long time if one has not considered where the forever should be.

At rest is never a rest without first asking if rest is everything you are advised. Think upon this, and you will be famous in the house that awaits all those who seek a name for themselves there.

FAMILY VALUES

One day, a man went to the home of his girlfriend and asked her parents if he could marry their daughter. The mother was unhappy with this request, as the man was not right for her daughter. The father was also unhappy, as he knew his daughter and her partner and thought, 'They are not right for each other.'

Time passed, and the couple decided to marry without her parents' approval. They went to a place where they could be married without anyone present to share the union and thought, 'This is best for us, as we know best.'

Again, time passed, and others in their families, though unhappy at this choice, supported the couple and made sure they felt loved and welcomed in their homes.

A friend called one day to say, "I have seen your mother, and she is not well, for her mind is seeing bad things coming for you. Will you be all right if I ask her to bring her concerns to me, for I see they are caused by your decision to marry without parental approval."

The couple said, yes, they understood and would be pleased if the person could help the mother understand that their love was stronger as each year passed.

A time passed again, and the mother was even more concerned, for her daughter had stopped calling and asking if she was happy and willing to come to the stores or spend time at home. Wondering if this was to last forever, the mother said to her husband, "Why is our daughter not happy with us when we only wanted her joy?"

The father asked the same of his children, and they replied, "Because you have not approved of their marriage, and they are happy with one another and in love. Their love is at peace and happiness, and we wish we had the same as they do, for they found one another, and we have not."

Listen all those who deny love, for in denying love, you are denying the ones who love. Be at peace with their decisions, for their life has a path to follow that is given at the appointed time—a path that has fruition if allowed to be of itself; a path no one should interfere with if they are called to approve the love of two people for each other.

A seeing of this fruition is a seeing of time. And a seeing of time is a seeing of family values given to those who made their choices in love.

TRUTH ALWAYS COMES OUT

'The day is going to be long,' thought the lady, who was often early and sometimes late.

She called a friend, who said, "Make sure you ask your phones to be quiet on the day of your visitor, as you will not want to be interrupted."

The lady wondered about this and decided to do as the friend suggested and ask for the day off work, for someone was coming to interview herself and her husband for the newspaper.

The day arrived, and it was just as the friend had said: talk flowed, and the phones remained silent. Joy was in the house at last, for the man had been in the news for something he had done that was secret, and it had been brought into the homes of the world, who read and ate everything up.

Time passed, and the story came out. The lady was awestruck, as it had been a nice day, and all of a sudden, the cries were louder than before!

"Why has this happened?!"

"What has to be done?!"

"Why cannot this house have its time in court?!"

For the magistrate was the journalist, and this journalist wrote the truth—not the lies that had been said by others with deception and a willingness to destroy their own hopes for victory at the polling booths.

The day was won, but not by those who came against the lady and her partner, for this was their day—truth at last!

Aforementioned trials unfolded, and soon the house was made well again; their hopes and faith had brought this about, and now they were singing songs of joy!

A song of joy sung at the end is better than a song of distaste sung at the beginning. Be sure not to trust those who have their own victories in mind, but trust those who suffer in silence, for silence has truth in it.

Unjust cannot be made just in the day of sincere attack; instead, it must wait for its own day—and that day is now.

SEIZE THE DAY

The day was beautiful and wonderful to behold in the many places it rose in. The called were full of joy, as it was a day the one who they looked to had made, and it was a new day when everything was afresh.

They took the day and made it a long one with many gifts in it; they went to the beach and to the shops and to the fun places where children could play, and they talked to one another and called each other friend—and it was good!

They chose this option, as it is a choice for those who seize the day—for a day seized is a day believed in, and a day let go through unbelief is a day lost.

Those who lose their days are not called to see the sun in their lives, but the night, and the night has much to hide—for those who live in the night miss the day; feelings are also colder.

Live in the day and let it be your light, for light is the best place to be in—a shoulder is always there.

MAKE SPEECHES QUICKLY

A manner of speaking had arrived at last. The one who wanted to speak thought, 'If I can say my speech well, I will be an advocate for others like me and can be their spokesperson also. Then I will have something good to do with my life, for what was taken from me has not been returned.'

The hours passed, and the time came to speak. A working person arrived and listened; it was as if the speech had no end, for over and over it went, and the person was not interested in what was said.

The man shook with caution at his mistake. He had wanted to be a spokesperson but was, instead, a poor spirit with sadness that shone in his words.

He laughed gently to himself, saying, "I have been a fool again. Why would I not just say this, or this, or this?"

Another laughed also, for they had not made the same mistake, instead working with the understanding that not all needs to be said. A wonder unfolded for them and not for the other—for, in being verbose, one is also boring to others.

Make your speech quickly, and you will see people listen, for listeners are also talkers, and no one likes to listen for too long without saying something wise—or so they think.

Quietness has much to say.

DO NOT RESPOND

The lady had a new and wonderful life! It was better than it had ever been, as her new friend in life had made it better; they had such love for each other that he made her shine with happiness. She wondered if it could be taken away forever, as she was so happy: 'Could it last?'

The way ahead was perfect, and she had trusted in the power that cares for her to make it this way—for she had waited many years for the power to send her partner to her and waited for *the one*.

The one was a man of importance who called into his own house another lady and made her important. He did not tell his closer lady, as she was *the one* for him also, but he needed the other—for his was an important job that had much to do and be. And he loved it and thought, 'I am so important, I should have the life of an important man, and this is that life—one with deception.' Or so he thought.

Time passed, and it came to be that the one he called into his house made it known that this man of importance was hers and no one else's, and she caused his fall—for he was so important that her testimony made this newsworthy—and the media loved the story, as it had a fall within it.

More time passed, and *the one* stayed with her man, as he was *the one* she had waited for and made callings into the universe for, and he, surely, could not be this man who had so sorely betrayed this waiting?

He made amends and kept his ways tidy for the rest of his life and made it up to her in ways they were joyous in again; the ways were made of travel and fun and love and laughter and reminded them of how they were before.

For, before the fall, the man had already made this promise to himself: "I will marry this woman." And marry her he did, for she had been so good to him, and he now knew she is *the one*.

Life has many callings in it and not all should be responded to. Listen and learn all those who read, for one day your life may have a calling you should not respond to. If you do, be sure it is one you are prepared to live with the consequences for—for not all callings end well; final outcomes are often final—forever tainted and never again as important as before.

OPEN THE DAY

The small animal was looking for her friend. The friend waited and waited, and still, the small animal did not find her.

The friend had waited all night and was calling, "Where are you, friend?" A little day was coming if the friend did not arrive, for the friend made the day much better. They walked and walked and looked at things and said things to the earth and to each other—the friend was the best friend in the world, as no one else had a friend like this!

The friend had been there every day, but when the friend's family took the friend on breaks, the day was small. 'Was today to be small also?'

Alas, the day was, for the friend had not come. Worse still, the friend was happy, and the dog was not.

'My own home is not as friendly as my neighbour's house,' thought the dog. 'If I could live there instead, I would be taken on breaks and know what the outside world is like, for I have never travelled or been anywhere.'

Time passed, and soon it was time for the friend to return home. The dog was so excited and knew it was soon, as her feelings told her so! She ran and played, and called to the earth, and made friends with the sky; the whole day was full of fun as she waited for her friend to return.

At last, the car arrived, and her friend jumped out and shook off the journey, running and playing with the dog. They walked and roamed and talked to the earth and to the sky, and they made it known they had missed one another by biting each other in fun and rolling on the ground to wrestle.

At last, the friend was home again, and things were normal; for this time, the friend had nowhere to go—for a time had arrived when the friend's family could go nowhere themselves as a virus was living in the world.

The friends were so happy, walking and walking and talking and living each day as they normally would, whereas the family were unhappy at not being able to do anything they normally would.

They walked some days and talked most days, and looked at their phones and the box with pictures, and opened wine and drank it, and listened to each other's stories of boredom.

If this day you are in lockdown, remember to do as your friends with fur like to, if you can, and walk and walk and look at the earth and the sky and wonder at the day—for the day still has much to give those who have nothing else in their lives to do.

In fact, the day has more to give than anyone knows, for the day is a gift and has much to open—yes, even a day in lockdown.

Forever is a long time when the day is not there. Find the day and open it, for forever is found within it.

NIGHTS HOME TOGETHER

Soon it was evening; the sun went down, the lights came on, and the night came into being. In the night, everyone was home and rested, for the day had been a long one with much to do in it.

They called people on their phones and talked to each other and watched television; it was a relaxed night, for tomorrow was the one day of the week when they could say, "Hooray—it is the last day of the week, and we are free to do as we wish!"

The day arrived, and they did as they wished. They relaxed in front of the television and called on their phones, and made food, and wrestled with what to do with the day they had, which was many hours.

One said, "We can do this."

Another said, "We can do this too."

Another said, "I want to do this."

So, they all did something different, and at the end of the day, they watched television and ate food and made friends with each other again—for the day was one each had enjoyed and done what they wanted to do with it.

To do this is not a crime, for the day is made for one person to enjoy as they choose to, and every person has this right: to choose what to do with a day.

For those who say someone else must do what they want to do in a day, is not the way to win a friend. Instead, the way to win a friend is to let them be free with their day and return in the night, for the night is much better to be together than the day; the night has times that can be against those that live together in harmony—should one choose to be of the night.

Live, therefore, with the choices of the day and remain with one another at night. Called into being are those things that make your days safe, and called into being are those things that make your nights *home.*

Forever called into being is the day; after all, it is the day that is the gift—for the nights have dangers.

THE POWER OF JUSTICE

One day, a father was walking with his son. They came upon a fine-looking place to stop and be waited on for lunch, and they made their day into one of friendly banter. Time was on their side, as they were both young in the eyes of the world and both had their health to be thankful for.

Just outcomes were also theirs, for they had won a battle against an enemy who had stolen from their home and taken much from them in the way of their infamy and fears of failure.

For fail the enemy now had, and a terrible *sincerely sorry* had come to them. And now the pair were cautionary no more—for they had won, and they had more money than ever before the day their enemy tried to take everything from them! At last, they could live and enjoy the day given to them by the power that calls for justice.

If this day your enemy has stolen from you wrongfully and left you without recompense, wait for the power of justice—for it is a power that has no boundaries other than law. And law is just.

HAVING EACH OTHER
The little bird had fallen from its nest and was lost in the world it knew nothing of. It was alone and afraid, yet kind to itself at the same time: "I have fallen and am lost, but I am also well and can manage if I can find a place to rest that is safe."

The little bird walked for a short way and found a nook in a rock where it was safe from the wind that blew it from the tree.

The wind was powerful and had much to say in its howling's. "*Wooosh,*" said the wind, and "*Hooowl,*" said its friend, the thunder that rolled and lightning that struck.

The callings of the storm took it away to other lands, and the little bird looked out from its nook and saw the day and the shining light above.

'I am safe,' thought the baby bird, 'and stronger than I was, for I survived the storm, and it could not find me safe in my hole of protection. I feel that if I can stretch my wings and make them flap, I can do something I didn't know I could do.'

The little bird did this and worked itself up to the top of the tree, where it found its brothers. They were all afraid, as they had weathered the storm in the tree, and it had pounded them with branches and twigs that hurt their wings.

They called out to their sister, "Help us, for we are broken and cannot fly as you are. Bring us food that we may be stronger, for our beaks cannot eat, for the fear is still within our hearts!"

The little bird who flew called back to her brothers and said, "My blood, you are not to fear, for I will go and find food for you and bring it back. Rest and take refuge, for the storm has passed and will not return this day."

And this is what she did.

Her brothers grew strong and eventually left the nest. They all flew together and laughed and sang, for their happiness at being free knew no bounds; freedom was theirs, and they had each other—for in having each other, they had survived!

When one falls from grace, another can help lift the other up. Forever, this has been so, and forever it will remain so.

HOME FOR DINNER

The day had much to do, and the one who had to do it all was overwhelmed with how much work there was to do in such a short time.

'How can I achieve this without making myself under the weather with stress?' thought the person. 'I have to do this and this and this and this—goodness, how will I do it all? I am just one person, and no one else can do these things, as they are mine alone.'

To make sure the person could get everything done and get home on time for a nice dinner, the person wanted to be at work earlier than usual. The person had a key and would not disturb the alarms, so the person went early, and much was done before others arrived to make the day busier than it could possibly have been if they hadn't come to work.

The person made sure she was able to give everything to everyone who asked—for early risers are good workers, and good workers are early risers; early risers have the mysteries of the day unfolded before the day unfolds its mysteries.

Be ready, therefore, to leave early and get home to dinner before the late evening when late risers arrive, for late risers miss their household's supper time, and supper time is when households should dine together. Forever it has been so, and forever it will be.

TRAGEDY IN PLACE OF VICTORY
The new hour was, at last, here! The woman had brought herself to this hour as one who cannot see ahead but knows it will come. The hour was one of victory, for hers had been a time of trouble and sadness. And much had been said to the one who had been the cause and to those who had made it eventuate—at least it was so in her heart.

The hour was a shallow victory, as much was lost, including her own fame and fortune—for her own fame and fortune had been years in the making and lasted just a short time. Worse still, she had not made the problems that happened, but had lived with them, for her own needs were more personal: a companion and a lover and a friend was all she needed. The worth of his wallet was second to all those attributes—but it had been nice while it was there.

The ones that took it away were their own enemies, for they had made sure it could never be returned as it had been before the problems. And, in doing this, they made sure their own homes were in danger—for this was the hour the world would know the truth at last: the man had done no wrong apart from being lustful at the wrong time with the wrong person. But those that came against him had been vengeful and had made calculated destructions of his name that were illegal and had no morals.

The world was, at last, told of this and now turned against those who had made the man a laughingstock and taken from him and his wife their own happiness and health and financial blessings given by the power that has this ability.

This power has not ever been open to thieves in the night, and now turned its force against those that had robbed its cared-for people, and they were now the laughingstock, now the ones suffering in the anger of the world, and now the ones whose homes were prior-convicted.

A lesson here: do not raise the hand of evil against another unless you are prepared for your own home to experience the same fall; for this is the gift of those that do this: a tragedy in place of a victory. Forever it is so, and forever it will remain.

THE CHILDREN
Whirlwinds made the eagle fly higher and higher. The causes were far below on the earth that groaned with howls of wind and rain, and the challenges of the one that brought the troubles to the world.

This one was not the bird, and not the storm, and not the howls of anguish from those who seek the power in their lives, but the children who wanted their world to be more beautiful and more clean than it was. And who wanted more and more and more than they could know was possible—for the world was fallen from the way they wanted it to be.

They wanted heaven, but the world was not heaven; it was the Earth, and the Earth had its ways. Its ways were not of heaven, and neither were its people. Its people were angry and hurtful to one another. They cried and lied and lied and cried over and over and over. Not all were this way, but most were, and, so, the world was the world.

A time passed, and the eagle flew over the world once more, looking down upon it. Cries had grown louder and louder, and people were filled with rage at one another and their governments, which tried so hard to please them all—a thing that is impossible, for the world has not this ability on its own without the power of the eagle to help it.

A time passed again, and the eagle flew over the world. This time the world had no noise in it—no threats, no bombings, no cries of children, and no living being… for they had finally made their choices, and the world was silent. Cries no more.

CHAPTER THREE

FRIENDS AND ENEMIES

HEAL YOUR HOMELAND

One day, a small animal went to the zoo and found its friends there. The small animal was so happy, for it had friends, and these friends were just like it was—small and round and fat. They all ate together and made their beds in the hay; they were all very happy, and time passed joyfully, for they knew their home was safe from angry animals that chased them.

One day a person came and took the small animal and placed it in the wild it knew it would find it difficult to survive in. The small animal shook with fear at this prospect and ran and hid from the world it did not know. The hiding place was quiet and, for a while, safe, and there was some food nearby that kept the small animal happy.

One day, another small animal found the place and set about making it her own. She nested and made problems for the other small animal, who had just left for a short time only to find her there on returning.

Quite a kerfuffle was made by them both.

"This is my house," one said.

"This is my house," said the other, "and I was here first."

"No, I was," said the other, "as you were not here before me, so you are last, and I am first!"

"This is not true," said the other. "I was here, then you arrived, so I am first and you are last!"

And so on they went, until one day they made a truce and said, "Let's share this place, which has room for both of us, as we are now like each other and can make this day a better one."

And so, they did this and were both happy, for in making peace, they found joy in each other's ways and joy in the added preciousness that differences make to the life of another with similar ways.

Forever it is, but never on the earth; a wait and then connectedness is abandoned to threats and days made terrible by the inability to share a homeland.

"Give it time," they say, "and it will heal," but this is not possible without love. Remember this and heal your homeland today.

FIND ONE PERSON

"Goodness," said the cockroach to herself, "I have made a new world, and here it is, at last! Forever I will be happy, as I can now be myself, and this is what is important. Everywhere I go, people hate me and want me dead, and now I can live alone and be myself, for no one will find me here."

Going to the shops to get mustard one day, the cockroach saw another cockroach, and they found each other very pleasurable to be with. 'Why not make special friends with each other?' they thought, and so they did and soon found themselves living together very happily.

The tree of mustard grew and grew, and soon it was much bigger than the cockroach wanted, for it covered her house with shade.

'I need to get help,' she thought, 'as this new mustard is too much for any one cockroach to use, and I can share it with others,' so she asked her friend to see if he could find others to join in their harvest.

The final order was that many came and shared in the

harvest of the two who wanted to be alone with each other, and the two realised they had much to give and were not alone or hated anymore—for they had found one other person to love, and in their love, they found many more who could be loved by them and loved back in return.

The lesson, therefore, is this: make a friend and find one person to share life with, and you will find your way to a day where your grown tree calls many to come—for a grown tree has much to give and, in giving much, it shares much further than a tree can do on its own.

A TRUE FRIEND

This day, a friend was going to see another friend. The friend had to ask a favour: 'Would the favour be granted?'

A kind person would say, Yes, I will do this for you immediately."

A person who was less kind would be more cautious and say, "I will think about it."

And a person who was not a friend would say, "I am sorry, I cannot help."

Forever the time was that a friend could call on another, and forever the time is that a true friend answers quickly. Let yourself be a true friend, for a true friend finds help for themselves in the day of trouble that arrives—for arrive it does. No one escapes. Ever.

REMOVE YOUR PLANK FIRST

A small trouble came upon the house, and no one spoke of it—for if they did, they argued—and so on it went, alone and unspoken, to keep everyone peaceful.

In time, the ones that had the small trouble called each other at fault and worked themselves into a day where they lost sight of how small the trouble was—because they had not talked about it in the beginning.

Time passed, and one thought to themself, 'I am not at fault, for I did not do anything wrong.'

And the other thought to themselves, 'I am not at fault, for I did not do anything wrong.'

...Each believing the other to be at fault.

Again, time passed, and the small trouble became larger and larger because each one thought they were not at fault and each one believed that the other would not speak about the small trouble if asked—for this is what was missing: asking to speak about the small trouble in a way that was open and candid.

Finally, the small trouble won the day, as it was now so big that neither could look at the other without seeing the plank in their eyes.

Today, if you have this plank in your eyes, see not the other person with it but yourself—for the plank there needs to be removed first before you can help the other. A day of remembrance when this occurs; a final will is here.

PRIDE

A wait was here, and waiting was not ever very much fun—for no one likes to wait—but the wait had to be waited on, for it was here.

A little wait was now in progress, and then a bigger wait, and then an even bigger wait—for the wait was waiting on another, and the other would not be solaced into ending the wait sooner than it should be.

And so, the other waited and waited and waited, and while they waited, they thought, 'I am waiting too long. Waiting this long means the other has no cares for my waiting or my feelings when waiting. And my feelings are hurt because the other has let me wait so long, and this means I should not wait any longer, so I will stop waiting and start living again.'

And this is what the human did—she stopped waiting.

Time passed, and the other realised they were no longer being waited on and was surprised! They thought they could make their lover wait, as this was punishment for being without love in their hearts when they came with a hurt that had hurt them and wanted answers.

The other said to himself, 'I have made a mistake and lost the one I love and who loved me, and now she no longer loves me. I have been a fool making her wait, for her worth is greater than my pride!'

And so it was that the couple broke their love apart, for pride had won, and pride is the last thing to go before a fall—for this is the way of the ones that have it: pride is not ever a preciousness, and forever it is a consequence. Let it not be yours this day.

FOREVER GIVING

Money had always been a problem for the lady, who did not ever have enough to be at peace with it. She needed much to care for her house and herself and did not have enough for this or for things like holidays and summer breaks to the seaside—so she went without for many, many, many years while others enjoyed their lives having more money than she did.

One day, she met her partner, who had a lot of money to spend and loved spending it. Her life changed, and she was, for a wonderful time, happy. And they were very happy until, one day, a large matter appeared that took the man's money away in an instant!

All of a sudden, their lives changed, and he was no longer

the centre of everyone's attention and no longer had everyone's heartfelt respect or wishes to be near him. The lady loved and cared for him while he made himself smaller and smaller in the eyes of the world. And she made him smaller in her eyes also, for he was no longer the man she met but someone she had not known existed.

He was fearing for his life, and she cared for him to ensure he did not need to fear. But his own ideas of himself, while they had changed, had not changed enough for his own understanding to see where he now was.

'I am important still,' he thought. "I can command calls from important people and make them answer me," he said, "and one day they will return, as I will redeem myself from this matter."

A time passed, and he was not happy with his lady, who asked so many questions.

"Why is this?" she asked. "And why is that?" she said. "And why do we not do this or that?"

He was tired of her and wanted to leave forever but could not, as he had nothing—not even a car to leave in. So he stayed and became more suffering than he actually was, for the lady cared for everything in the house and in the world and made him look better than he was. And the questions she asked were few when she actually had many more—as was right given the situation. But he did not see this and continued to be bigger than her, even though she owned much and he had little; she had work and he did not; and she had many friends willing to help, while his had left him.

He saw her fears and thought nothing of them, instead saying to himself, "She is not my partner anymore. I will leave as soon as I can."

And leave he did eventually, going to the city, which he loved so much that it had caused his downfall. And he went to those who caused his downfall and made friends with them again and again and again until, eventually, he went to heaven and met his wife there.

She had much in heaven, as she had made stores there also—a big house and many helpers who cared for her—as she had been great in life and had made her home in the heavenly sky into a great one. He saw her then as she actually was—a good planner and organiser, and someone who did good things he had not known of.

He saw her kindnesses, as the stories abounded in the heavenly realm, and he knew he had been one of them, though he had not known this at the time—for he saw only his own ways and not hers, and not her as she was but as she was not. And she was not his to call a friend anymore, for his house was not with her, and his house was so small that it had nothing to give to people with big houses.

Money means nothing when, instead, it is how we treat people without it that is important. And he had not treated people without it as she had. Worthy in many ways, yes, but not in the ways of the realm that awaits.

Give, therefore, to others and be a help to them, and you too will see a day when others come back to you and treat you as you should—even if your matter is large. Forever giving to be given in return, seeing others as they are, and being good to those who are good to you.

No one knows this secret except for a few, and few share it as no one listens with ears that hear. Be one who does.

SEEK LARGE VIEWS

Little windows see little views, but large windows see large views. The larger the window, the better the view. And the better the view, the better to see the beauty of the world.

The beauty of the world is seen through many windows, and not all are windows that have views. A window without a view is a window lost to the world in its seeing. A human needs views, for without them, a human cannot see.

If, this day, your views are limited by small windows, seek larger ones, for in finding them, your views will grow greater, and understandings will come that were not there before.

Only those who do not seek larger views grow in smallness, never understanding. But those who seek larger views always grow in wisdom and understanding.

Be a person who seeks large windows, for they are everything to the human who seeks to be with the power.

OPEN THE DOOR

'Many are called, and few are chosen,' thought the lady as she went to her door to see the visitor.

The visitor had knocked twice, and she let him in. He came inside and stayed, for this was now his house also.

Time passed, and the visitor changed the house so much that it grew and prospered and changed its windows to large ones. The visitor cared much for the lady and saw to it that she had everything she needed—even love.

One day, the man who loved her made a mistake and let another visitor inside the house. This visitor did not care for the lady or the man and made sure the house was devastated by the mistake. The visitor could not stay though, as he was not invited to. Instead, the lady, whose friend had stayed, cautioned her own self, and made sure she remained faithful, knowing that all would be returned.

And it was, for the day of the attack was over at last, and

instead, her house was prospered again, this time with things she wanted and had asked for but had not yet received as gifts. All the while, these gifts had been planned, and all the while, they waited for a time when they could be given, and all the while, she knew they would come—one day.

And that day is today, for today she has her monies returned, her fortunes restored, and her name given back—for today her friend has helped. The friend of all is a friend to you also. Make sure you open the door when He knocks.

IT IS DONE

Sincere apologies were unfolding. The apologetic woman had made an enemy of the friend's friend and had not been good in her ways with managing the matter.

Her own friend was not the friend people would want if they knew; instead, he was not a friend but an enemy who lied and was not nice. This friend wanted people to think he did not exist, when he did, and this was his way: to deceive and to use people who were deceived. This friend had no friends and was never a friend to anyone. His partners were the same, and they knew each other enough to know they would turn on each other as well. And turn they did, for they consumed one another and lived this way.

A matter is never a matter when one has the friend of all to defeat these enemies, for the friend of all did this long ago, and once done—always done.

Never fear, never doubt, and never cry, if you can help it, for your friend has all things in control, and you will be lifted to another day—one where your enemy is defeated.

GO FOR WALKS

Small animals were waking up and getting ready, for their mistress was also getting up and would take them for the highlight of their day soon—a walk!

The lady was always looking for ways to walk her pets, for she loved the journey herself. It took her into the best part of the day—the part where she was free of concern and free of busyness and free of trouble—for her mind went to the outer reaches of the world and made hymns to the sky, all the while being kind to herself and growing stronger inside in life and hope and freedom from all the things that can hold a person back.

The lady knew this and made her way quickly to the best part of the day. The small animals made their excitement known by jumping and running around her legs and getting in her way.

She laughed, as this was part of the fun of the best part of the day—being with the animals that brought her joy, for their own love was that she loved them too.

They called to each other and went to the place to wait for her to manage their walk. 'How exciting!' they thought. 'We love this part of the day most of all, as it is when our mistress loves us back!'

And so, they all went for their walk and returned happy and in a better place than before.

If this day you are in need, be like the lady and go for a walk. And if you have an animal to take with you, make this animal your companion, for you will both return joyous.

LOVE HAS NO CORDONS

The day was wet, and it rained and rained upon the house and its inhabitants. They were warm and dry inside, for the house was one that was safe and secure. The people slept while the rain fell but did not get wet, for the roof saved this from happening. And even the small animals slept safely and dryly inside, for this house loved everyone.

Meanwhile, there was one outside. It was not warm, and it was not dry either, for it had no home, only the seat on the veranda where it slept because it wanted to be close to the happy house and not its own—which did not love or care for it as much. Its coat was thick, and it was not bothered, but it wished it could be like the others and be inside, especially this day when the rain fell so hard that it bucketed.

Try as it might, it could not get comfortable or find a place out of the wind, which also blew. It turned and twisted and made sighs, for it knew it was different from the other animals that slept inside. One was its friend, who got everything and was happier, for it knew it was loved so much, and another was a smaller animal that no one knew was in the house, but it knew, and that's all that matters.

Time passed, and no one went to the larger dog outside to ask if it was all right. No one sent extra blankets or extra bedding to keep it dry and comfortable, and no one gave it more food to keep it warmer in the shivering cold.

Try as it might, no one came, and no one gave it any attention, for this was not their responsibility. They gave it love in their own way, saying, "Hello, good morning, how are you?" each day and giving her some food they had to share, but not the kind the other had, which she wanted so much and, in her body, needed—for she had a surprise coming for everyone—a puppy, maybe more!

She looked at herself inside and sighed again. 'My family is not caring of me, and this one is, but not as much as I need them to be. Will life ever change and get better?' She sighed again. 'I am not the dog I want to be, for I want more and do not know how to get it. What can I do?'

She looked at the houses and the cars and the people and searched through the roads and byways for a better life.

And, one day, it came, for one day, a stranger took pity on her and said, "I wish to have this dog for my own and will ask my neighbour if this can be so, for she has been my friend for so long, I cannot bear to see her so lonely anymore."

And this is what happened: the dog had a new master, and her children had their new masters. And now the dog was happy, for she had done what few orphans have—she had won the heart of a kind person and been brought inside to the warmth of a home—a home with safety and security and love. And this is the day the cordon fell—for the cordon that held her back could do so no more. And that cordon was love, for love has no cordons and no sighs.

FRIENDS ARE A GIFT
The person was a good person. She had much to do and be and choose, and she tried to do and be and choose her best but often did not, instead doing and being and choosing unwisely.

More than once she said to herself, "Not everything I am, or can be, or decide to choose is right, and often it is wrong. Everything I touch goes wrong, and nothing much goes right. If only this had gone right or that had gone right, I would be better off than I am today."

Or so she thought—as she did not realise that her matters that had not gone right had been managed by a power that chooses these things. And the power had decided it was not the time for things to go right in the way of her finances or her partner in life, as the power had much to teach the lady about herself and her ways, which, while good, were also fragile and lifeless and had coldness where there should be warmth. She had been rejected as a child and had placed these stones in her heart as a way of being safer and more secure in herself.

And so, the years passed, and she was taught many things about herself.

One day when she looked inside, she thought, 'I have not

been the friend I should have been, for I have done this, and this, and this, and not been at peace with other people who are no longer my friends. And I am worse off for this, as no one calls, and no one cares that this has happened to me as a person of light. I need to be a better friend and make my peace known more.'

This happened, and the power looked upon the lady and gave her hopes and dreams beyond that which she imagined possible, for she was now worthy of having her imaginings answered as she was now a friend to those who were friends, not just to those who were not.

And this is the lesson: be at peace with those who you call friends, for theirs is a gift from the power, and the power has lessons if the gift is turned away. Forever it has been this way and forever it will be this way.

Today, make your friends into your own self. Do this, and your friends will be with you always... forever and ever.

ASK FOR HELP

Quickly the sun rose, and quickly the manager's requests came: "Can I please have this" and "Can I please have that."

There was little time for the work already there, and the new requests were many, and the lady thought, 'I am tired and did not rest enough last night and feel overwhelmed with the requests that keep coming, but I must do my best, as my best is better than another's best, and this is what I like to be—better than another at working and achieving that which can be achieved.'

So it was that, one day, the lady had no rest and no patience and snapped, "I cannot keep this pace up and do everything that needs doing. I cannot, as no one can, and if I could be of more assistance, I would, but I cannot. I am sorry."

And the manager stopped asking for that which she could do herself and stopped wanting that which she could do herself. And the lady was happier, and so was the manager, for she realised her day was busier and went much faster than it otherwise did. So much was achieved, and much was had by those who had it.

Today, if you are too busy, ask someone to see if they can help, for in asking for help, you are saying, "I cannot do it all." And no one can, for we all need help—every one of us—even those that can achieve more than others because they have many abilities, and especially those that have much to say and be and do.

Ask, and you will receive.

MADE WHOLE AGAIN
A much-needed adventure was, at last, on its way. The adventure was one the seekers needed, as they had not been out for a long time and they both sought adventure; sincere asking's had been made to the power who controlled lives on earth, and the power had granted their wishes at last!

The day dawned, and the couple made their way from the city to the countryside and walked amongst the flowers and the trees and the beautiful nature reserves. At once, they felt refreshed; at once, they fell in love with each other again; and at once, they were brought to a new day—one with less trouble in it than before.

A call was made, and they were even happier, for the caller said they had won the money they wanted for the defamation against them! A joy unknown was felt in their beings, and their trust in the power, who held them for months at home in hiding, was released into the world with shouts of joy and laughter and callings of praise.

"Sure enough," they said to each other, "we were made a laughingstock to the world, but this day, it is we who laugh. And the ones that laugh last, laugh longest and loudest!"

Trying to be what you are not will always bring about an

issue you cannot resolve without help. But being what you are not in the eyes of the world will always bring about the truth—for in truth, we are made whole again, and in wholeness, we are made happy and live forever with the power that made us whole.

Today, if someone you know has lost face, let them know you support them in their time of lies against them. And be with them as a true friend would, even though you may not know the truth, for it may be they are telling the truth, and have the last and longest laugh without your being part of it.

A time for everything and a time for joy is here—believe, and you will see.

A NEW DAY WILL ARRIVE

Forlorn, the new worker sat, considering their feelings. 'I know I am better than this outcome,' the worker said to themselves. 'I have made a mistake from the start when I wanted something I could not believe in, and now the belief is already departed.'

Working through the situation, a call came. "Why have you made this choosing?" asked the one with power. "Why have you not made this one instead? Why have you made yourself larger than me when you are not this way according to your level? Why are you never on my side?!"

Trying to be an assistant when an assistant is not wanted is not easy. Today, if you are one, remember this story, for it has no ending for the worker who wants to be wonderful but is not able to be.

Trying to be what you are not is sometimes a loser's way out. Think upon being what you are regardless, and you will see a new day arrive; indeed, it comes today.

MASTERS OF NOTHING

Funny creatures were making fun of each other on the video. They called out and ran about, and jumped at items placed next to their beings by their owners, and cried when they saw the vegetables.

"What is this item that has come to be mean to me?!" they said—and leapt, for the item frightened them!

A man gave one a cucumber to video the reaction, another a carrot, another a pineapple, and another a funny man that looked bad. All the creatures were afraid and ran to hide from that which they made fearful in their minds and their furry bottoms.

'Living like this is not funny,' thought the creatures. 'We are regal and princely and should not be made fun of!'

So, one decided she would take care of the situation and wrote to the news media that published their videos. "Look," she said, "you are making us fearful when you do these things. We are kings in our world, and you are making the kings look like clowns without the costumes."

Already, the news media was laughing. "Why are you so serious?" the owner asked the representative. "We are kings in our world also, and we find the idea that you are kings amusing and like to poke fun at you with your ways of princes and princesses."

"Fine," meowed the representative, "but don't expect us to like you anymore than we have to, for we will bite and scratch and kick and friend your cautions against us in ways you will know who has the last laugh. And then you will know who the real kings are—for we only come when we wish to, dine when we wish to, live with you as we wish to, and friend you as we wish to.

"You are just our servants, and never will you have the longest laugh, for while you make us momentarily afraid, you must always watch for us and our revenge. Beware, therefore, masters of nothing, for the cats are your owners, not the other way around!"

This day, if you frighten another because you think it is amusing or harm another because they react in a way that is amusing, further your cause by ensuring your enemy is truly defeated, for if not, they may return to rule over you, and you will be at their calling for destruction upon your life. Then you will be the one who never knows when they may exercise this power or how—for written into the world is this law, and forever it is so.

A PLACE FOR EVERYTHING
Lightly, the small withheld fly went into the house and the night, where it buzzed and buzzed and went everywhere it could to be a nuisance to the lightly sleeping person—and the one that snored all the time but did not know, for the fly had made his snores quiet.

Flight is good when one can fly, but not good when one has wings that burn out and cause much-of-an-ado about the one that can fly around and around and around. Too soon, the poor bug went to the blue light that beckoned, and BANG-ZAP-KAPOW, it went to heaven.

On the way, its windswept blowing hurtled by worthy masts of true-blue steel that cause flashes in the day and brushes in the night, and the fly caught up with others, also brushed aside by steel and burnt by sun and flushed by water, and passed them, going quickly to its destiny as a frightened burnt creature of habit—though little had changed for it as wings arrived once more and plumes of feathers like flight-filled hair.

"Enough!" said the human, who woke the dream from its slumber and nudged the snoring happiness-person next door. "That fly has been too much this night, and now it must go. I will shut the blinds and spray it with hairspray, as that is all I have."

"So long as you do not spray me," said the monied man. "You know you do sometimes, and then I have sticky hair on my head which has small hairs like the fly."

Sure enough, the bug was sprayed, and sure enough, the man was too—both stuck to each other, and no matter how hard the laughter shook the room, the fly was stuck on the man's short hair.

To do this to a bug is to do this to a man, for even bugs have life, and life is to be brought to the light to care for. The day man shoo's instead of sprays and leaves instead of stays, is the day the life inside a house blooms once more.

For life is cool to those that hurt its managed beings, even sticky flies that have hair like yours; hair that has much to say about its owner, for hair has DNA—and that is life.

A place for everything, even that which annoys.

SINS OF THE PARENT

Sighing, the lady wanted to die. 'My name is wonderful, but my hopes are carried through the wind, and now my life is over—I am nothing—and I am afraid of my partner, who lifts his hands to me nearly every day.'

Wanting to end her life, she did. And her partner found his own life lost also: "My wife has left me for another, and I cannot go there, for if I could, I would bring him to his knees!"

Hearing this, the hopes of the Father who loved him also withered. 'This man has no love for me or for his wife,' he thought. 'I will see him in prison for his crimes, as this may hurt his manner and make it into one that wants more from others than their hurts.' And so the Father informed on his son, and the son was imprisoned for life, less 20 years.

Learning his fate, the son moaned with shy sadness. "My

God, my God, help me!" he said to the life that hears. "Why have you done this to me?!"

'Why?' answered the man's head while his heart remained silent. 'You are not a human being who is loved, or who loves. You are a monster who has a rage so terrible that you acquit it against the innocent. You are deserving of your name in the paper that states you are guilty.'

"Guilty?" said the child inside the man to his elder. "I am a person of innocence also; it was my father who started this shallow anger, and my father is the one who should pay, not I!"

And there is the story, gentle people: the sin of the parent is not always, but mostly, the sin of the child. Forget this, and you procreate the shallowness's of your manner of being on them.

Forget ever being repaid, though, for that is another story to be shared—one so terrible that awaits those who are not sentenced in this life but in the next. Friend it, and you friend a fate so worse off that you will wish you were in jail with your sons or daughters… a pipe dream.

THE MEANING OF TIME

The day arrived, and now the moment. The called-for being was called into the zip-lock bag of darkness and then into the gate of blue skies and love that never ends. The being passed through the gate and into the blue sky above and went on and on and on to another place where time stood still.

The white light expired and left to get another to bring to the blue sky, and then another and another and another. After all, this is what time does: it brings those who are ready to the new way of life and those who are not to the darkness of space, where time has no meaning—for time only means something to those who live in it.

SILENCE IS NOT THE WAY

Silence was the key, for this day, everyone was silent. No one knew what the other was thinking, for silence was upon the house, and the house was silent. Try as they might, the ones who were silent could not find a way out of the silence.

Forever, they stayed silent.

Forever, they thought to themselves, 'I am misunderstood. I am not loved. I am not cared for. And I am not happy, for this is why—I am misunderstood.'

And so, the week and the month wore on, and still the silence remained—for silence has its way also.

Silence has not ever won hearts, or minds, or witnesses to hearing. Instead, silence remains silent. That is why it is never a true saying, "I will remain silent," for in silence, the only winner is the noise that never comes—a frightened outcome for all.

Staying silent is not the way. Forever, it is so.

MAKE THE DECISION

One day, there was a small, furry animal that went for a walk on its own. It went to see a friend, then another, and another. And the ones it went to see were interested enough to say, "Hello, it's good to see you here," and so the small animal visited and laughed and played with them.

As the day wore on, so did the animals' friendships, as they wanted no more laughter and playing, instead wanting rest. And in this, they walked away from the furry one, saying, "Goodbye, we have no one left to see now. Please leave us so we can eat and relax, for this day has more to give than your barking at us."

So the small animal left and went for another walk somewhere else.

Shining lights came and lifted the animal into their machine, which purred and hummed with gentle noises.

"Why are you alone?" they said. "Why are you not at your own house?"

The furry friend answered, "Because my parents are not speaking to each other and have not made me their interest in this day. Swine have instead visited and made friends with me, and so have the mooing friends, so I have made friends with them so I can pass the day wisely instead of wasting it.

"Forever I asked my family to come and play, and forever they ignored my beckoning, so I left and entertained myself. And now that you are my friends, good people, will you be happy to stay with me today?"

"No," they answered, "for we have worked and are weary also. Go home and see your family instead, as they need you."

The small animal thought about this for a while and decided to do as they suggested.

Upon arriving home, the family shouted for joy and said, "We are here and have waited for you to come and bring us back together again! Why did you go and leave us to our own selves when we needed you to bring us back together?"

Kind person, be this day at one with all those in your home, even your pretty, furry friends, as the home is home for all, and the ones that leave may not return as this one did. For, in making your home quiet with hurt, you also make it absent with friends of all kinds—even the furry ones.

Today, make this decision: be happy.

CHAPTER FOUR

TIME AND CONSEQUENCE

NOT SOMEONE TO CARE FOR
One day, a hurt person was so hurt that she organised someone to hurt someone else so she could feel better about herself. The other person did this in the news, and, so it was, the lady who was hurt felt better about herself. She laughed and thought, 'I am the worthy one who now holds power over the one who hurt me, and he will hurt me no more!'

The day wore on, and the lady found that she was not happy enough with her actions and decided to do more to hurt the one who had hurt her, so she called and called and called and called and called and called everyone she knew who knew him also.

They were shocked at her actions and soon realised they had misjudged the person who had made the news and lost his job because of the woman and what she had said and shown the media. Little by little, they said to themselves, "We have misjudged this man and this woman, and now the man has his life lost, and she has hers won. We must change this wrong into a right!" And so they did.

The day came when the man was uplifted in the media and the woman was made low. The man was so happy, as he had not expected this help when others had been unkind towards him, and he created a new day for himself and his wife—who he had made sad through his actions.

The other woman knew herself to be wrong but still claimed

she was right, but no one listened, and no one cared—for she was not someone to care for.

If this day you consider harming another for the hurt they have done to you, remember this lady and think twice, for in the end, you too may be uncared for.

MADE TO WIN

Soon a gay day came for the household, and they were excited! Would their animal win its race? A drive to the city was made, and they arrived feeling happy and soon saw that their horse looked very well indeed; she shone, and her happiness glowed from inside out.

Lifted by this, the household made its way to meet the other owners, who were also very excited. True sayings were said to one another when they each said, "We think she can be at the finish." And so it was that the little animal won and made all her people so happy, they cried with joy!

A final word here. The horse is the best friend of humankind. The horse has many abilities, and some are to race, for a horse that races is one that has a spirit inside that calls to action its very soul—a soul made to win. Forever, it has been so.

Wins are wins, even in the horse world.

SUGAR

Sugar had much to blame. "I am fatter than I have ever been before," said the woman of older-age-than-before her marital ability far exceeded that of now. "I have gained weight around my waistline and am frumpy. I do not like this, as this is not me, so I will make it go forever!"

But nothing works forever, not even a workout. And, so it was, the woman tried hard and hard tried her, for her own hard self-drove her on and on into the bleakness of forever being unhappy with her wrongdoings with wine and sugar.

"Too late," said the sugar. "I have my own thoughts about this also. You must pay for eating me, for I am your own self that loves sweet things and wine to drink."

"Listen," said the lady, "I will make an agreement with you. You love me, and I love you, so let's wait for each other sometimes. You can wait for the weekend, and I will wait for it too."

And this is what they did: one waiting for the other to come and enjoy each other's company... and it was bettered, for the lady lost her middle, and the sugar lost its cravings for her.

For cravings are better left alone to themselves, and so are ladies with bettered lives who want too much of everything they like. The day you know this tale, you will also know it is coming to meet you—if you wish for it to be your partner in life also. Friend sugar, and you friend a mate for life.

SWEETNESS

Sweetness is a little way away this day. Sweetness is a gift made blessed by families and friends; sweetness has its liftings; and sweetness has its lifelong bettering's.

If this day your heart has lost its sweetness and found its harried self with no one who cautions you to be better in your ways, find your own trouble and loss—for loss will be found if this is your way of being with ones and fives.

Always, this is the poorness of life. Always, it is your own sacrifice to that which is inside. And always, it is better left unsaid—for this is sweetness: unsaid thoughts and unsaid actions; actions without thought for your own future... a future of sweet nothingness if you do not choose this option.

THE BOTTLE

All the house was silent as it slept, except for the one who owned it. This person was very tired and very cautioned about her work, for she had a busy role that required her attention all day long. So, the night was a time when sleep would help her, but sleep was not ever there, for her mind was too busy with, "Tomorrow I must see to this and see to that, and do this and do that," for she loved her job and enjoyed the pressure.

But it was not this that made her wake in the night; instead, it was her hangovers from drinking on arriving home to unwind from the day.

Heads are sore when alcohol is there, and the mind does not treat its master kindly, and for this reason, the lady lay awake not realising her troubles were not from work but from her relaxation. Had she known this, she may not have drowned her anxieties in a bottle of something nice. Instead, she would have made her exercise a priority and left the bottle for times with friends and family.

If you are like this lady and have a job that causes great busyness, remember her story, as one day it may be yours also.

FIND THE GRIT

Called into action was the man who had left something undone; he hurried and hurried and finally made the deadline, not realising it was this process that he had made for himself.

Forever willing but not ever trying hard enough had been his issue. He met needs just in time, and just in time was the way he worked best—or so he thought. He transferred all his energies to meeting the deadline, and just in time, he made it!

Willing this cause into action had made him more weary of the task and more lacking in its enjoyment than if he had worked harder at the start and in the middle, instead of leaving everything to the end. And he questioned whether he could complete the next task on time—as he had left that one too late also.

Flying through it, he made the deadline, but it was not a work he was pleased with. 'Forever, I am not good enough for this work,' he thought. 'I cannot do it as I want to, and I am not willing to keep trying, as I never get it quite right.'

Forever is a long time, and forever is time to start tasks early and keep workloads even so they are not all at the end. Forever can make them right, and forever can make your life choices right also.

Work in the beginning, the middle, and the end, and you will receive the result you hope for. Find this grit, and you will find your own house raised.

ASKED FOR LUCK

Soon it was to be a new "good morning," and the morning was one that had much to do, for the risers were very earnest in their plans for this day.

'Will we sell the car?' they thought. 'We need to sell it as it has some things wrong—nothing so great that we are fooling the buyer, but we need some things to go right, for much has gone wrong lately, and we are weary of this way of luck.'

And so they went to meet the buyer, who had also risen early, thinking to himself, 'Will the car be what I need? I know it has some minor things wrong with it, but will there be more? I have had some things go wrong lately, and I need some luck that has not been at my home.'

And so it was that they met and exchanged the sale of the car, which was a very good car for the price, and everyone was happy.

Today, if you are experiencing luck as having left your door for another, think not upon this but upon the luck waiting to greet you, for luck has this way about it: a sending from the one who has this ability to send... if asked.

BE PRESENT

For the one who has everything they need in life but no one to care for, a day can be a long day and the night even longer. For the one who has little in life and many to care for, the day can be a long one and the night much shorter. For the day is time spent in life, and life has much to do and be done.

If this day you have much to do and care for, wait for the day to bring you a gift, for the gifts are there if you look: a smile, a follower who cares, a little animal who seeks yourself and no one else, a child whose eyes see into yours, a fear allayed when a gift arrives unexpectedly, and a window that comes with being a good helper to others.

See the day not as one to pass but as one to be present in, and you will have the days of your life extended by fruitfulness and prosperity. Assuredly, it is written.

VISIT

The family had a wonderful expedition and left to meet its unknown outcomes, and the vehicle was full of excitement!

"Let's do this and let's do that," said one who knew where to go. And this is what they did; living the shared experience of an unfamiliar area through the one who lived there.

"I know what will make them happy," she said to herself. "They need joy after what happened one day ago and one year later. I will be the driver, and they can be my houseguests, who I will make feel at home."

Soon, the day unfolded with much joy for all the people.

"I love this," said one.

"And I love this too!" said another.

Too soon, the day was complete and never to be held tight again; too soon, it had run its course; and too soon, it was never to be had again.

For everyone to know this is important, as a day has its friends forever and its friends for the day. And this day, you have yours and we have ours, and this day, a friend is asking you to visit.

Be uncomfortable if this is what visiting means or be without the day appointed if comfort is your first priority—for sometimes visiting a home is not as comfortable as your own and can even be uncomfortable. But what is comfort compared to shared experiences that last longer than the discomfort it cost?

Forever being inside is not the way to lifted states; forever being outside is—comfort or no comfort.

THE GREATEST GIFT OF ALL

Soon, the managed home went to sincere, very hoped-for wellness. And soon, the unmanaged home left for its worried-about day trip, for the people there were always fretting about what to eat or wear and forgot that these things are not the day but the night—when worries come.

The day has no such hazards if the people who wake to meet it leave them alone to be forgotten, for the home has much inside it when one thinks it does not have anything. Look, and you will find things to be and things to hold and things to love—for it is these things that have meaning.

A dress has meaning for a day; a family has meaning for a lifetime. And it is this that is richer than many dresses and many fine things to eat and wear. And wear they do, for they have no love for you when they are worn, or tired, or old. But the ones you have held do, and it is this that is the greatest gift of all: people.

Be one today.

A-FAIR

'If, today, we go to the show, we will have a wonderful time, and we will see the fair and all the sounds of the show and be in a wonderful place full of joy,' thought the couple, so they went to the local show.

The day was beautiful, and the sun shone on their faces as

they sought the attractions and made faces at children who laughed at their happiness and joy at being alive. Around and around went the ride, and around and around went the couple as they spun and made shrieks of surprise at each turn.

'Some days are wonderful!' they thought to themselves, "and today was one, for today we were free of our cares and made every moment special.'

The day turned to night, and soon they were home, weary from their joys and adventure. The night was sold to the television and, later, to sleep. And in the morning, the couple woke and remembered their day before.

"Do you recollect this and that?" they said to each other. "Did you see that animal with the beauty in its eyes and body? And did you feel the small, quintessential feeling that came when we shook hands with its mane? Was it not a thrill to be there? Let's go again next year!" And so they planned to do this.

One year later, they set off to the show again, and again had a wonderful day, remembering all the things they had done the next morning. And so they decided to go again the following year.

This time, the day was not so fun, as it had anger in it that morning.

"Why have you not got my wellbeing in your heart when you say these things to me?!" accused one to the other.

"And why have you done this to our home?" said the other to the first. "A friend has been secretive with our relationship in a way that you have not shared with me, and I need to know why you have done this to our home and our lives!"

Cautioned by each other's anger, they went to the show that day and found it was not so fun and that the day was not one to be remembered—or even had again.

This day, if you are someone like this couple and wish to keep your days wonderful, do not do anything to harm the other or their love for you, for you risk their anger and their hurt and will be in a place where a fair is no longer a fractionally happy place. And for a fair not to be a happy place, there is no other place that can be happy.

TAKE NO OTHER THING
When a small animal wants something, it sees what it wants and says to itself, "I would like this, and so I shall have it," and takes the thing it wants—a berry, a fruit, a whirlpool of fun, a gift from the day which was made.

When a human sees a thing it wants, it says, "I want this thing and will take it"—a fruit, a caring smile, a shallow whim, a frightened child, a marriage, a life. And the human takes it and makes its own self happy.

Today, if you see something you want, be like the small animal and take that which the day gives but no other thing, for in taking a thing the day does not give, you will be found and punished—if not by another human, then by the power that punishes and rewards all.

Caution is required in life, for life has a way of cautioning those who take without being allowed to. See and believe.

SAID PLEADINGS
And so it was that the whole farm was so wonderfully blessed, for the rain had come at last. It had been many years since the last rain, and the farm had withered and crops had failed, so the farmer leapt for joy as the rain came down! The rain was a good rain and had much life in it—for life is in rain, and the farm sprang to life. Everywhere the life grew, and it grew green and luscious.

'At last!' thought the farmer's wife, 'we can eat and be happier than we were when it had not rained for so long, for in not raining on our farm, our lives were not happy and not blessed.

And today we are blessed! Blessed with love and laughter and happiness, for the rain came after many wishes and said pleadings, and we are now far more solicited for our markets than we were before.'

Today, if your farm has not had rain and your home needs it, plead for it and ask for it, for the knowing power will hear and answer. And in being answered, your house will be a happy place once again—for rain has life in it, and rain can come every day... if asked for.

PROTECTED FOREVER

'Forever' was on the mind of the small beast that walked on rocks outside the window of her home: 'Forever I walk on these rocks and make fun of them, for they were not mine to walk on—and yet I do.'

The owner of the home had placed the rocks in a garden so the man's saucy pet would not walk on the flowers. There were so many rocks that it was called a rock garden, and it had sincere prettiness—for it had rocks and more rocks and even more rocks—and then some small plants that would grow into larger ones in time.

The rocks laughed also, for they enjoyed the dog walking on them.

"Look," they said to each other, "There is that black creature again that comes to say hello to us. We like it because when it says hello, we move a little and know we are also alive in this beautiful world of the home we live in—far more beautiful than the quarry or ground we once lived in, for now we see the sun rise and set. And enjoy the visits of the black square animal and the small fiery beings that flit on us in passing through the wind.

"Today they are quiet, for the wind has died down, but tomorrow they may come again and see us as they pass."

For the fire that passes this house has no place to stop and goes to the next, where it always stops—for the wind has magic in it—magic to make rocks into life and send life into rocks, and to make small animals furry and round with happiness, and large animals brought to winning ways with wings on their heels for their owners... should their owners wish to have one.

The wind can also bring fiery beings to homes that have no protection from them.

Today, make your home protected from changes wrought by fiery beings by protecting it from the blowing winds that come from the north. Those who understand already know what these winds are; those who don't must learn about them—for in learning, their houses will be protected forever.

DIFFERENT PAGES
The day had been considerably challenging, as the people were in touch with only themselves and not each other. The worker had been challenged and was tired from the week. And the one who worked, but not for wages, was wanting more from the other—who had nothing left to give.

The worker wanted to be cared for, for this was her problem—she didn't feel full of life this one day. The one who felt she should be more considerate of his feelings was not tired, nor was he called upon in stresses related to the work of the challenged one; nonetheless, he had worked and was satisfied with his week and its bearings.

The bearings of the other had much more weight and, in this day, more than she could bear—for every day had been relentless for weeks and months on end. And this day, she was too tired to even care for the racing horses she loved so much—and he cared more about them this day than she did. For all of this, they were on different pages in different places, and neither knew what to do about it.

If this day you are feeling this way for a day or two, do not be concerned, for always these times pass and the friendship returns once life and its energetic moments return. This is the way of the worker and the non-worker, often in different places at different times. Forever, it is so.

MAKE FRIENDS WITH THE DAY
Work knew it had to be done, and the person who had to do it knew this also. Still, it was a day when work could wait because more important things also needed doing.

'The small beasts that enjoy my company and the morning walk must always come first,' she thought. 'They need me, and I need them also, for we have this day to call our own, and then the employer can have the rest.'

They set off, and along the way, they stopped to look at the fruit on the trees, the ground with its grasses, the sky with its blue, and the scorching sun as it started to rise. Already the heat was great, for this morning it was summer, and summer in the country where the group lives is very hot—so hot, the sun reaches its peak at twelve o'clock and again at four o'clock and again at eight a.m.

The day grew hotter and hotter, and the small dogs were lying on the grass waiting for the lady to come home from work and be with them again. They knew not to walk around too much, as this made them hotter, and heat has a way of making everyone weary—even the smallest of the animals, who loved to jump and run and chase birds away from the house.

The sun looked down and saw the meaning of life—as the day passes quickly, and all those in it considered the next day and the next day and the next day and the month ahead and the year ahead—but never the day.

The worthy ones, the dogs, looked at the sun and said to it, "We love you, sun, for you are on time today, and we know our times also. And this is the time to enjoy your rays and not do too much, for work has a way of working itself out and never needs to be overly considered."

The only consideration of a day is the day, for a day may not ever come again if the one who works too hard does not take it and make friends with it. The day is a given day not to be fruitless, it's true, but also not to be all things to an employer, or a manager, or a worker that needs help. Instead, it is made for the one who takes it and makes it their own.

BUY THE TICKETS

Flying was now able to be undertaken, and everyone was so excited! It had been many months since anyone could fly, even the air people who went here and there in the planes where they worked. Already the ones that could buy tickets were buying them, and already the tickets were running low—so low, no one could afford them as the prices started to rise and rise and rise.

One man, who had many free aero points he could claim, looked at the costs and thought, 'They will go down in a while, not up as everyone thinks.'

And so he waited and waited and waited until, at last, he needed the tickets so badly that he bought them as they reached their height—for higher and higher tickets go when everyone flies, and higher and higher they go when the place that everyone flies to is at a special time of the year, when everyone wants to travel there.

In this, let the lesson be known: if your kindness needs to be forever made kind to others, buy the tickets when you see them, in case they are more expensive, or perhaps not there, when the time comes to leave for a wonderful holiday to a faraway place that has much to do and see.

Flying is for the flyer. The payment is just money that comes and goes, and no one has control over.

RELIEF FROM TROUBLES

The wonderful manner of being relieved is a manner so many want—relief from trouble, relief from issues, relief from financial matters that cause sleepless nights, and relief from the burden of worries that have a way of being much more troublesome than they need to be.

The lady felt the relief work through her mind when the man called to say, "I have made a new consultation arrangement that makes me this much money in just one day! We can now live again, for at last, the power we asked for help has given its own workings in our lives and brought the help we asked for—just as you said."

"Wonderful!" cried the wife, who was outwardly overjoyed and inwardly relieved—for relief was the real gift given by the power: relief from troubles that come to people who cannot resolve them themselves.

Relief is that which all humans crave, and relief is only possible from the power that brings it on the wings of many asking's. Relief is a relief, and relief has much to live for.

A friend once said this: "I will give you this relief. If you can ask it for yourselves, you will also get it—wait and see." And see you will.

YOUR TRUE FRIEND

Try as they might, they could not bring themselves to ask for the help they needed. A manner of being was inside their own frightened selves, and they knew they could not get what they needed without committing a crime. So that's what they did—

they stole from a neighbour and brought their thieved goods home and hid them in a secret place only the other knew of.

Once a day they checked it and found it there, and then asked each other, "How will we make this property our own—for it is not, and we want it to be."

At last, one had the idea of gifting it to another person who would give good money for it. And they took the money and had enjoyable times with it, until it ran out and they were back at the beginning of the swing of stealing from neighbours.

Again, they stole from another—and again—and again—and again. It became easy to do and to make money from, and they made names for themselves as thieves able to steal anything wanted by someone else.

Too soon, they were arrested and turned over to the jails that had awaited them since the beginning of their spree.

The jails greeted each one and said, "We know who you are, for you have been sent to us to create in you even better thieves and better liars—and we wish to make you one of us!"

Too soon, the jails had their intentions met, and the two thieves learned much about life and death in the cells their friends lived in—for stealing is the small start to a larger issue that has much pressure and few friends in the final hours.

Trust, instead, in the power to bring your needs when asked, and you will know your true friend, the universe, who waits for all to ask it for gifts.

CHAPTER FIVE

THEN AND NOW

QUIET LIVING IS BETTER

Living quietly was not how the person who had life inside their eyes wanted to live. "I am not going to be this way," the person answered their inward desire for excitement. "I am living today and not thinking of anything other than me."

So life requested a meeting: "I am excited to hear you want to live day to day, as this is the way to live life in its fullest possibilities, but I am concerned you do not want to live in the way of bliss and contentment, instead wanting existential joy from extreme ways of living."

"Yes," called the writer back to her old self, "I did want that but now see it's not the way and wish to live each day with blessed bringing's, instead of self-reached outward goings of fruitless searches for answers and people and boys and wins and sodden messy days of drinking to get drunk.

"Life is more than these outcomes; it is otherworldly beliefs with held up waits and calls for wonders and prayers answered at last. And, in between anticipating the presents, living in the day, and resting in the night, and finding small gifts to open instead of fighting for them."

Quiet living is the better option; a lifelong challenge is over, and no suffering is attuned to it. Believe, and you too can overcome your inner whining for adventures with consequences unknown except to your own selfishness and personal enmity. The writer knows.

LIVE IN THE LIGHT

"Less is more," the lady said to herself as she went about her matters of beauty. "I can seek needles and glowing skin in ways that hurt, or I can use the light of this world in a way that is healthy." And this is what she eventuated, for her skin looked natural, and it glowed from morning until late at night when she placed the red light on her face.

The red was deep in colour and made deep impacts into her facial plumpness. And when it was red, it was very red because it was infrared. And infrared is the light that generates the light in this world, for light has many aspects to it; light can reach faraway places in ways humans are only just beginning to understand.

Light has much travelling to do, and travel it does, as it can travel through the deepness of space and into the worlds of here and far away where others live and use light too. Light is itself a living thing, for light has knowledge that sees all beings and what they do in it.

When it is not light, when it is lack of light, the healthy people are asleep, and others wake to make their nights fun in ways the light cannot see and does not want to see—for the light has life within it that is healthy, and the night has darkness that is not always healthy.

Today, if you live in the daytime, you are at one with the universe, which gives its light for all to be in. And if you live in the darkness, you are not, for your home has no light in it. Be at once opening the curtains and the windows and doors, and let the light inside your body, for light can reach your very soul and change the way you are—from sincerely depressed to wonderfully happy.

Live in the light and you will not ever be unhappy enough as those who live in the darkness. Friends, light cures.

WORKING TOO HARD

Wondering what to do with his own life and its callings, the man worked hard. And the harder he worked, the less pleasure he found in his day—for his day was long and had no moments in it to make his world a better one.

His marriage was failing, and his family was almost gone, for they had left many years ago when he was younger and made more of an effort to say hello… as he'd also said hello to another who was not his wife.

In the end, the man had no one who cared for his wellbeing. No one who said, "You need to lose weight as you are getting fat around the middle in your old age" or "You need to get a medical check for it is due, and you need to do this as you will be safer if you do" or "Here is a good thing to do as a family—let's save and make plans and go, for we will love the days and enjoy being with one another."

And so it was that the man put on weight, and didn't get his medical checks, and didn't go on family holidays. Instead, he worked and worked to fill the empty space in his heart left by his lovely wife and children—and the one he had loved also but who did not love him anymore, for he worked too hard for her to suffer as well.

Today, if you are wanting to work long hours, think upon this man and his story and decide if this is also something you wish for—for in wishing for it, it is easy to win, far too easy. And too many win this life of all work and no play.

Trust in the power to send what you need when you need it, and the things you need will come in their time, even much money worked less for—for in working too hard for it, it simply vanishes in other ways.

LOOK FOR ANOTHER

Work has many wonderful moments—moments when life is good and everyone has much fun with people who are not their family or friends. Work is also a greater good, as it gives the worker the sense of being a contributor to another step forward and another task accomplished well.

It is a good day when a worker feels good about their trying's and achievements. And a wonderful thing to take home to share with family and other possible employers who may want the same kind of achievement in their organisations.

Today, if you are not happy in your job, look for another, for in looking for another, you may find what you are looking for, and your new employer may find a wonderful worker who enjoys their job. A matter of excellence for all concerned.

GROW AND EVOLVE

This particular day, a small animal went for a walk with her mother, and they travelled along the roads near their home and looked at the birds and the clouds and the fields and the grasses and wondered at the sky and all that is in it.

"Look at this," one said to the other.

"And look at that," they each said together.

The walk took them to another place along the route—one that was not walking or looking, but one of sensing the world and its wonders.

The wonders are many if you look, for the sky above has

much to see if you care to wait on it to open its doors to your soul. Forever it goes on, and forever it works its way through the cosmos—forever and ever. And forever is vast and forever bottomless, and forever speaks of worlds far away where life also lives.

For life has a way of living and growing and evolving in the light that shines on it. Evolving in ways that understand rather than change shapes, and in ways that make wealth of knowledge good rather than bad, and in ways that bring forth new life into worlds that await this life with joy, not hunger or pain.

This world has not yet reached this place, but it will one day. When that day arrives, be ready for it, for you will need to be.

BEWARE OF GREAT WEALTH

"Look," said the man, "I hold this world in the palm of my hand and own it, for I am a success and others are not as successful as I am. I have much wealth, and they do not. And I have much prestige because of my wealth, and they do not. I am the owner of this world and everything in it—I will buy whatever I want and make the world I own into my sought-after home where people will come and pay respect to me."

And this is what he did: he worked long hours and travelled across the globe, buying works of art and expensive, sought-after objects for his large house in an exclusive place where others with similar views lived.

"At last!" he said to himself, "I now have everything needed for people to pay me the respect I have earned through my own cleverness that far exceeds that of others. I will open my doors, and they will come."

And come they did... all the time. Every day, many people came to the man's house and used his generosity so they could have a good time. They used his money to eat and drink and be merry with, and they also used his car and his pool and his friends, as his friends were the same as he was—wealthy beyond imagination—and they worked hard at being friends with the wealthy people so they could enjoy their wealth also.

Then one day, the fairy tale ended for the man and his wealthy friends were no longer there—they had left because their money expired in a stock market crash that ended their fairy tale lives and took their friends away.

The still wealthy looked at each other and said, "They were not like us, for we are the clever ones. We kept our money hidden from the world that looks to see where it may devour it. Instead, we went about things quietly and made little of our money, letting it hide in places only we know of. And we made it work for us, so our children and their children may enjoy it—not some strangers who we do not know or care for."

If you are wise and come into great wealth, learn from this knowledge, for it is the ones that have old money who kept it, not the ones with new money. For money has a way of choosing its friends, and friends have a way of choosing money, old or new.

Beware of great wealth, for it makes fools of those who abuse it. Give instead to family and those in need in secret—for in secret, the light sees what you do and will reward you with more than you can spend in a lifetime.

WORTHY OF YOUR GIFTS

The nice, worthwhile thing was waiting. It had a call placed upon it, for it was being sent by a good friend to another good friend, and it was a lovely surprise for that friend. That friend had been a good friend for many years and had been a close friend as well, for the friends had worked through much together—cries for help, laughter, and joy, and all things in between.

The friend who was sending the gift had known the other was in need today, and today the gift was coming at last. The choices that had been made were wise choices, and the falls were bad, so the friend needed all the help possible and was also worthy of it.

At last, the call came. "Who is this man we need to work for us?" they had asked each other. "Is he the one we read about in the paper, or another who has behaved so well after the fall that we have forgiven his bad behaviour that caused it?"

Forever, they had called him a friend, and, for that moment, he was not—for that moment, no one was. At last, a decision was made—he was a true friend who had been good to their cause, and so they called and asked him, "Are you available to do this work for us?"

Asked for this, the man said, "Yes, I am," and leapt for joy, for his whole life had melted away when he fell, and now it was back! "I will do this and do it very well," he told them.

And, so it was, the gift arrived—the gift the friend had sent to the home that needed it and had asked for it. For in asking, they had been sincere, and in asking, they had endured much, and in asking, they had received—and received because they had asked.

If this day you are in need, ask for your needs to be met and wait. And while waiting, meet the needs of others as much as you can, for in this action, you will be made worthy of your gift from the power who gives.

NEVER GIVE UP ON DREAMS

Hurt and sore, the animal rode itself forward in the work of its life. "Why are they so mean to me?" it asked. "I wish to be a good horse and a very fast horse, but, today, I am not good enough, for my own excellent, healthy body has a hurt in my forelegs, which is not what I need right now."

And so it was that the horse ran poorly—so poorly that

everyone thought, 'This horse does not have anything to offer us' and sold their shares.

Already, the poor horse was happier as it went to the paddock to get well. "My legs are much better, and I feel very well," said the mare to herself, "so much so, I will run faster next time and win."

And this is what happened—the horse was the best horse in the stable, and it showed on the day it won the very big race.

The one owner left was so happy, as she had bought all of the horse and given it to a good trainer who knew how to train mares with sore legs. And this was the lesson: never give up on dreams, for dreams can come true in the strangest of ways.

QUITE THE ONE

Swiftly, time went to see the next person it wanted to take home, and swiftly, someone went. Swiftly is the best way to travel to the next dimension, unless the person does not know of the power that takes them there—for not knowing has its own matters of attendance to bear.

'Quite the one,' thought the lady as she worked her way towards the pretty-coloured windows in front of her.

'Quite the one,' thought the one waiting to receive her.

Already, they came to one another, embracing as they fretted no more about being apart. *Quite the one* is the way of this sensation: the one that waits to greet and be the one to all who come.

ONE PERSON

Forever, the water weaved its way around the rocks and on to the ocean, where it met with other waters. The waters were changing in time and in forfeitures of soiled matter, for the water had travelled for a long journey and had met much on its way; soiled wastages of man and beast had greeted it, and so it carried it away—not wanting those that lived by it to be troubled by the forfeitures of their own wantingness.

"So," the water asked the next wave, "what are we to do with this wastage made by the humans who I passed by?"

"Well," said the wave, "let me take it from you to another place I know that collects it in one place and holds it there for animals to visit and be captured by its interestingly fraught ways." And this is what the wave did, taking the wastage to the centre of the ocean, where many beautiful creatures visited and became entranced by the moving wave they wanted so much to entangle with.

One day a boat came and brought with it a net to catch the animals caught in the muddle of waste, and it caught so many that it held its breath, not knowing if it would be able to keep up with all of the beautiful animals in their distress.

"What can we do?!" cried the people on the boat. "We have no way of helping every beast that comes to see the wastage of all the world and cannot stay here all the days and months and years."

So great was their distress that they called the world and its leaders on the phones they had and showed them videos of the matters of waste from their countries.

"Look," said the leaders, "we need a solution to this problem and do not know what it is. What can we do to make people stop throwing their waste into the drains and runs of water where they live? We have asked and asked and asked, and yet, still, they do it—not all, but most are without care."

Forever this issue has been, and forever it will be, unless it starts with one person: YOU.

SEE THEM

Poor people have much to be happy about, for they do not have to be concerned about money and relationships and friends and being better than other people. Instead, they have their own friends and family who love them so much that they give their days to helping each other survive. And survival has a strange way of making people happy: happy they lived another day, and happy they made each other happy by helping one another to be fruitless in their destiny—but alive for another day, nonetheless.

To be truly unhappy, one only has to look at those who are so sad with their lives that they cannot see the beauty in the world they live in, or in the rooms of their houses, or in the food on their table, or in their own eyes that look back with clean teeth and friends on their speed dial.

These people, who are so unhappy, need only to know they are so cursed they should not live anymore—for their own lives are nothing compared to all the people on their video messages. The same video messages that do not ever show those who are very poor. And, in being very poor, they are blessed, for no one has ever told them they are not successful enough to warrant breathing the same air as another.

See them, and you will see yourself and your own unhappiness in another light.

POSITIVE THINKING

Poorness is a true quietener, for people who are poor have no money to live in ways that are hectic and fast. Instead, they plod through the days and months and years, always wanting but never getting. "Trust," they say to each other. "Trust that one day we will be absolutely fearlessly raised up to be what we should be—children of the power who lifts those that trust."

And so it was for the power couple, who lost everything in

one hour, that their hectic lives became very boring and very slow, and over the months they worked without the heavens opening with abundance as it had been.

True sayings were said to each other, and true sayings were said to the power that wrested their lives from the darkness that enveloped them.

Time passed, and on one day, in one hour, all things changed because they trusted; for in trusting, they believed, and in believing, they won!

Positive thinking gets positive results. Forever, the human can think blessings into being. All it takes is winning the fight of the mind over what the mind sees. Imagine, and you too will win the fight of the poor and find your wealth in the wind that brings it.

FRIENDLY AND HELPFUL

Many had made their names in the workplace the lady lived in and had passed on to other roles within the organisation. This day, the lady hoped it would be her fortune also, for she had worked hard and been helpful and made friends with everyone in her new role that would end soon.

She looked at the advertisements and made the decision that she must try to earn more, not knowing she would in time anyway... for her own writings would be her fortune. Instead, she tried to earn her way forward on her own, without any help from the power that cares for her. So she applied for another role and another role and another role—never winning any because this was not to be her fortune. The day would bring another instead.

"At last!" she said to herself, "I will be my own self and have time to travel and see the world while earning money from my books, which young and old people alike enjoy."

And this is what happened, for this is how those who lift

their minds and hearts to the power each day earn their keep: by being friendly and helpful to others.

REDEMPTION FORESHADOWED

Work had become a wonderful joy at last, and the man had much to say and do and be, for at last he had made his own way in the world and been appointed as a chairperson to a committee that needed his knowledge and fortuitous ways with people who do not want progress on their doorsteps.

And so it was that they listened and learned from the man who had once been made lower than the lowest by the woman who had complained against him using lies.

And this is how those who trust are redeemed—lifted at the time of the lifting being possible. And this time was the man's own special day, for he had waited and hoped and trusted that all would become clear for his way forward.

"I will ask the power that helps to help me," he said in his mind and heart every day. And he asked and asked, and, at last, his asking was answered. He was so happy, he called his wife and said, "We are whole again at last!"

"Hooray!" said his wife. "I knew today was the day because I wrote about it this morning!"

And so it was that the day foreshadowed arrived at last—the day of the last day of the week—the day when those that are blessed have a night to remember, for today is that day.

DIFFERENT OPINIONS

The one thing the older man wanted from his lady was that she kept her views on everything to herself; she was too opinionated and too bossy all the time. So he looked further and found a small, thin girl who looked up to him with eyes that said, "Come and see me some time." And he did.

He went to her and found her pleasing and wanted more and more. They were happy with one another living under the lady's roof, and soon it became clear they wanted to live under their own. And this is what they did, leaving the lady with opinions and interesting things to say behind, sad and unhappy.

Time passed, and the man found the thin girl less and less attractive. "She does not know me like the one I left did. She knew me enough to say interesting things with a point of view I had not thought of before. This one just listens to me and nods," and he considered what he had done.

Forever, he regretted his misunderstanding of the lady, who grew in stature as her views were shared by others who now listened to her through her books, and he called her to say, "I was so silly. Can you forgive me?"

The lady thought about her foolish husband, who was not himself when the thin girl called, and said, "If this is the last time, I will see if you have changed, for your given day is over now and you are also well in my eyes again." And so they returned to each other's arms, for this time both knew the other to be their true love.

A wake-up call for all who read: not everyone who has an opinion you don't like is an enemy; instead, they can actually improve your own views with theirs.

BE A TRUE FRIEND

Summer arrived, and the weather was sensationally very extremely heated—super weather for superimposing each other's many called for requests onto the beach of their dreams.

Wonderful days were spent in each other's arms, as the couple found one another once more in the surf and the sun. Time was not important, and the summer days passed on holiday in the beach areas of Sydney, Australia.

Well-heeled people walked through the malls and shops and bars and very expensive areas with nice homes, very happy and relaxed—and very tanned. Everyone remarked, "It's good to see you. We've missed your smiles and happy comments that make us laugh. You were always fun to be around—we love your stories told with eyes that bring mirth and arcane attritions of hilarity."

'Funny,' thought the lady who they referred to, 'you were not as friendly when I was here last time or the time before. Instead, you dismissed me, for my husband was fallen, and now that he has remade his life and we are well with money once more, you want to be friends. True friends remained through these times, and you were nowhere to be found. Yet here you are again, wanting friendship when you offered none when we needed it.'

Cautioned, the couple left the beach and went to the countryside where they lived and to the friends who had stayed by them through tough times when they had found these people genuine with their callings and meals with one another. All through the tough times, these people had been generous with their caring and their time and their money, and the couple knew they were people worthy of being called friends.

In life, few are true friends, and many are friends with causes behind their friendship that, if failed, fail their friends. This day, if you have a friend who falls, be a friend to them through their fall, for you never know when they may be lifted in front of your eyes and make your false friendship a regret.

THE CYCLE OF LIFE
The little worker was busy making bundles of sticks into a nest— a stick here and a stick there, and here another stick and there

another stick. Soon it was done, and the bird flew into the nest and laid her children apart from each other, so they were not crowded as they grew in their shells.

Forever and ever, the bird sat on her children, keeping them warm from the cool air and heated at night. She made calls to each one, saying to it, "I am here, and I love you. You are my child and no one else's, for you are made of me and I of you."

Little days passed, and soon the eggs cracked, and the babies came into the world and cried, "We are hungry, mummy. Where are your gifts of food for our mouths?"

Quickly, the mother bird gave her children their goodness from the earth below, and quickly they wanted more and more and more—always hungry, always wanting more.

After a number of weeks, they said to their weary mother, "We are big enough to fly away and will do this now," and this is what they did, leaving the nest built with sticks from the labour of their mother and never returning.

Called into the new place without children to feed hour after hour, the mother left the nest, also never returning to it. And, as winter passed, she wondered about her children and if they were well and cared for in the cold days and weeks and months.

Spring came, and again she made her nest and fed her children and cared for them until they left the nest, never to return. And years passed with this cycle of birthing and caring and resting, over and over and over.

One day, a man looked into the eyes of the bird as she rested in his hand, dead from having lived and bred and flown the world over, and he thought, 'I wonder why this little bird died when there does not seem to be anything wrong with her?' And he dropped her body into a hole in the ground, burying her to see if this would help the tree he had planted there.

In time, the tree grew very large—large enough for birds to

nest in it and raise their children to fly the skies to watch over the world and its people that rush here and there but never fly as they do. And so it was; the world turned and time passed, and still, life continued—for life must forever fall to the ground and grow into new life for the world to continue turning as it does.

Written in time is this process, and so it is *the cycle of life*.

MADE READY FOR HUMANS

Trees made forests, and forests made the world, and the world made its own health from the trees and forests. In time, the trees were lost to fierce winds and forest fires that made them into pieces of wood on the floor of the forest.

The forest worked over the top of the trees fallen to periods of fierce weather, and time carried through the air into millennia... Always growing and falling... and falling... further into the ground to become petrified as coal and other good things people use to keep warm and heat their food and make their homes and visions for the future of humankind.

A gift is the wood fallen in time—one the power has given so that the children of this world, no matter where they live or how, may find fuel for their bodies from the ground where it fell. A friend to all, and the cycle of life made ready for humans.

PRECIOUS PAPER

For the words to be written, the paper needed to be made. The workers busied themselves cutting the tree and making the pulp so the paper could be written upon. Tried and tested was the method they used, and there it was—paper!

Precious paper. Paper to work with. Paper to write with. Paper to send into the future for others to read to understand the past.

Writers sharpened their pens with feathers and pencils with

slate and made sure their words expressed that which they had learned from life.

Winters passed, and the writers did too—into the ether of the time they wrote of, so historians could look upon their world as it was and make sense of it for others to understand their own world of time.

Paper.

THE POWERFUL PEN
A written implement for those who want to be more than they are is the pen. The pen is a mighty blessing, for it has power. And power is understanding, and understanding is power.

The pen.

WHEN SPOKEN WORDS FAIL
Sincerely sorry, wrote the man to the lady he loved. *I am sincerely sorry. Sorry, I did not love you enough in the hours of my being free from your presence. Sorry, I was not alone. Sorry, I did things I knew you would not like. And sorry, I lied.*

The lady read the letter, which was on pretty paper with a bow and written in nice ink with a fountain pen the man had bought to make his effort at writing more special, and her heart melted thinking of how much his trying had involved to get this special piece of kind message to her.

While he had not made the paper or the pen, he had made the effort to send her a special gift that would sell his good intentions to her. And she made a place for the paper in her carefull drawer where she could open and find and read it when happy she had been forgiving—and when things were not so good as they worked through his betrayal of her trust.

Windows into his heart were in the words, and in the words,

she found his love and never lost it, for it was written into her heart on the paper of love and ink of worlds gone by. And forever she treasured it.

Pen and paper—a way to be at peace with others when spoken words fail.

CHAPTER SIX

LOST AND FOUND

AT ONE WITH EVERYONE
The sun looked from its room and found favour in what it saw—the dawn was beautiful across the oceans and the lands of this world—and the world knew it, for the world was so beautiful that others in the universe found its beauty to be such an attraction they made sure they visited regularly to ensure it could never be lost in time as other worlds had. One had made its forests dry, and another had made its seas red, and another had made its future bleak with wars and troubles, while another had made friends with everyone that came to it, trusting they came in peace when they did not. After all, the world was not something that anyone could make. And the ones who made such worlds were always busy making others with changed delights to see what they looked like and if plans could be improved.

One day, a boat came to visit the world of humans and make itself known to them. The boat was large and had lights across its bow, and it said *hello* with the lights. The people below took to their planes and shot at the boat, wounding it slightly but enough to scare its passengers away.

"These people are warriors and do not wish to be friends with other worlds," they said to one another. "The warriors of this world are fierce and wish to destroy each other. We should leave them and see if they can make their world a better place, for not all are warriors; some are peaceful and wish only to be friends."

So, the boat left and passed by from time to time to see if the warriors were defeated by the peacemakers. Alas, this was not what they saw with their magic windows from space. Instead, they saw the peacemakers friendless in the world of ferocity towards others. And that the ones that were fierce in power had great wealth that ensured they remained powerful over the ones that had none.

"Today," said the people from other worlds, "we should try saying hello again to see if their hearts have changed towards us," and so they waved their hands and said, "Hello," in words the people of the earth could see for themselves and know the intentions were peaceful.

"Hello," waved back the people on the soil of the nations. "We see you and thank you for coming to save our world from those in power who seek to wage war, for war has its own ways of making profit."

"Cheers," they also said as they drank a toast to their protectors in the sky.

'Well,' thought the people on the ship in the air. 'Now we can shake hands and make friends with these people who seek to be friends.'

And this is what happened: they landed and made friends with the world, for the world was at last ready. And, in being ready, they were ready for the power that enables light to travel fast in places where it is not seen by the human eye, and now the world was powered by the light and travelled through it to other worlds they saw and marvelled at.

For *at one with everyone* is the way this world must be before the ship comes that will land to see if you are ready for its wonders.

BE AT ONE

Choosing to be angry is never a great decision, and today the lady made it once more. Justice was there, but then it left and did not return, for no one likes a lady who is angry.

'Still, she is right,' thought one.

And another, 'Well, we did see this day arriving because we didn't create a day where we are in control of race decisions.'

And so it was that the lady, who had made her post to the Facebook group of people who owned a horse together, received their distain and silent, unheard support at the same time—for they too had been mad with the trainer, who had not said anything to them other than, "We race tomorrow", and not, "We could scratch"—but had not said anything in anger when it happened.

Today, if you are mad at someone, see that you are not angry, for in being angry, support is lost and people leave. But in being more political, people listen and stay, for they too may feel the same way but not be so forthright as to say it.

Forever being honest with feelings is a good day, and today, the lady does not choose to be angry anymore, only disappointed, and makes her case more wisely—a day of wonderous outcomes made true, for this is the desire of the power who guides even those that are angry: be at one with everyone.

BE KIND TO IMPERFECTION

Dying to someone's own hurt ways is living with hope, for the day one dies to being hurt by someone is the day they are hoped into life once more.

Forever, people will be imperfect, and the day one is perfect is the day one is forever plied once more with imperfection.

Perfection is not possible for anyone, so no one can expect another to be perfect in their fraught moments or in their tested ones. And testing is what the human can be. Testing to all; testing in views and actions and moments in time when their feet live in their own mouths.

Once a day a human fails, if not another and another—once, twice, three times. Yet few appear to realise this and, instead, believe others are imperfect and their own perfection is more obvious than it may be.

Only kindness is perfect, and in kindness, the imperfect human is perfect. Therefore, be kind to imperfect mentors and imperfect leaders and imperfect ruined men with vices and women with causes for anger. Instead, know they are imperfect forever and can be no other way, for only the one who knows the power of the universe can reach perfection, and even then, they may need to leave this earth for that to be.

Right therefore are all people, unless wrong in their own eyes.

YOU WILL NEVER BE ALONE
Signs had been asked for, and at once, signs were received—signs that all is well, all has a purpose, and all is forever made better.

Twice the lady had asked the world to be made perfect for herself and for more than just her own house, and twice the universe sent a good friend to be there in the days when no one else was.

Surely the kindness that has been made into friendship for someone who is alone, the sign is this: that you will always have at least one friend who is close enough to be a friend that is worthy of yourself.

And so it was that the lady, who was lonely always, had a good friend to care for her as she waited for a larger moment in time—one where her gifts were at last received and no more were the days spent working for money. Instead, they were spent alive in the world of travel and adventure and the knowledge that, if anything ever again is made poor for a reason, then, once more, a friend will be found to be a constant source of momentum toward the day when the wholeness is returned.

Wait, therefore, and you will know a gift is always received, as this is the way of the universe that seeks those who seek it: you will never be alone.

THE POWER OF WORDS
Swimming further and further and further into the solitude of self, the man looked inwardly and saw a man he did not know anymore.

"I'm not sure where I went, but I don't think this way today as I did yesterday. Where are the smart comments and the frigid replies?" he asked himself. "Now I wonder if people might consider what I have said worthy of their own understandings, for I have made a giant step into the world of forever thinking others are better than I am now. And now I want to be more like them—more understanding and more lenient on the views of other people than I was before my fall."

"Rightfully so," said his partner, the one who had taken him to this place. "You were not right in your thinking and writing on social media walls and made others unhappy with what you said, which, while right, was not written well. Instead, you write more carefully now and with greater consideration of the power of words."

For words are powerful; words can sting and pause a person's kindness towards another. Words have a bright light when put beautifully and a dark one when not so.

Forever, the words of the mouth and the pen are words that should be caught in considerations of others before being let out—for, in letting them out without consideration of others, sickness can also be let out. Of this, then, take care with words, for words can make even the speaker sick.

FOREVER IS AN ETERNITY

Sunny days lay ahead, ones with much to do and not much to do—much to do around the house and not much to do outside—for not much needs doing in sunny days, so fiercely hot, the wind burns the face red and makes legs tan so quickly, they peel.

"Right again," said the small, furry beast as it looked to the sun for answers. "You have made yourself hot, and now I have nowhere to go in the heat you have made, and my feet are sore from the hot stones and my fur glows with sweat."

The horses made their peace with the sun under the shade of trees, and the birds made their peace in the branches, but the small furry-mattered beast had no place to go, as her home's trees had not yet grown big and could not be walked under.

'I shall go to the river,' thought the dog, and off she took herself. Along the way, a bigger dog walked with her, and they made their plans for the sunny days ahead.

"We do not need our tall friend to bring us here when we can come ourselves," they said. "We like her, but she doesn't let us go to the edge of the river and walk in it as much as we would like, and we like the river so much, it calls our names every day to come and visit." And they went to the river and visited its banks, walking and enjoying their lives as free as birds and as well-cared-for pets of humans.

Swells rose and the wind blew, and the pets sought shelter in the trees next to the river, which started to rise swiftly.

"What has become of the sun?" they said to each other. "Where is it when we need its rays? Instead, we are calling for help on the edge of a swollen stream with no one to hear us cry to the sky!"

Choices had to be made—come and rest in the power of the world that awaits or try for the other shore.

Too soon the river rose, and too soon there was no choice left other than to go to the world that awaits them. Swiftly, a light came for them, and swiftly it carried them to a new world of lovely fruit and windows in mansions, and friends who laughed and made each day a wonderful one. Always, the pair were in shade when they wanted to be and in light when they wanted to be, and always, their coats were skimmed and clean and shiny, and always, they looked their best.

Once more, they looked to the world they had left and saw the tall lady leaning over their old bodies, crying. It looked so sad, and it was for the lady, who did not know they could see her sadness.

"Wait for us to come to you," called the lady's dogs to her name in the light that shone. "Wait for us to save you on the day of your own coming to this world, for you will not travel here alone. We found the way and will see that you find it also."

The callings made the lady's heart feel somehow better, even though she had not heard them, and so she cared for the bodies of her pets and made them comfortable in the ground that received them back to its warmth and coolness. And sometimes she visited them to say hello and share a rose with the place that meant so much that tears came when visiting.

"At last," said her friends in the new world, "it is time," and they went to find and bring the lady to the place prepared for her.

She was overjoyed to see her friends with fur and hair and

feathers and scales and frightening growls and lozenged meows. "You're all here!" she exclaimed. "I knew you would be!"

And so it is for creatures that travel into windows of light. And so it is for the human, though not all have someone to help them reach it, and not all can come—for if all could, the world that awaits those that seek it would be the same as the world that was left.

In this way, get ready, for you never know when a sunny day can change into a storm so severe that you are alone in a place with no one to guide you. Forever is a long time to be in that place, and forever is an eternity.

THE LIVING UNIVERSE
Sometimes a small matter can become a large one, and sometimes a large one can become even larger. For those who have matters that need help, there is a way of being helped that is much better than anything anyone can make for themselves, and this is to ask the world for support and the molecules for rescue.

The world has its ways of being worthwhile, for it can spend money and bring friends, and the smallest of molecules can travel through time to go ahead and find a way to bring back help, so it's waiting, ready for the ones that ask for it to be there for them when needed.

Always, molecules can travel and force themselves into places of cautionary wholeness, and always, little beads of light can change a circumstance for someone in need.

Today, if you need help or have a matter making its way towards your body or household, remember to ask the world for its help and the little molecules for theirs, for the little molecules are always moving around and can surround you with protection and defences you are unaware of—for molecules can be everywhere at once and nowhere at the same time.

Molecules are living beings also, and the universe is made of molecules, and all are in touch with one another. And the universe sees and wishes much for its creations—and those creations are yourselves.

You are not ever alone, and you are not ever without help—this moment and the next. Forever is not just a time; it is also a place.

COUNT THE COST

Lifted in size and stature was the man who made it his will. "It is my will that today I will be famous once more," he said, "for I was famous once, and once more I will be famous again." And he set about making himself famous once more.

He called people and made an appointment to be on the television news, and he said to the reporter who asked him questions, "I was made a fool in front of the world for no reason. I was made a mockery of by a woman who told lies to cover her own wishes for my job."

And the world looked and learned that the man at whom they had laughed so hard was, in fact, a benefactor of a woman who could have been jailed for what she had done.

'Today,' thought the woman, 'I am the fool. My name is in the newspapers, and my own house is surrounded by media who want to make me into their news story. Today, I will not be as I was yesterday when I plotted his downfall. Instead, I will be left forever in the wilderness, for I do not ask the world or the universe to help me; I only ask myself.'

And this is what she did: she asked herself for help, going here and there and not finding it anywhere, for, now, people were against her for what she had done and had made the man their friend, not the woman.

And so it was for the man, who had asked the world and the universe for help, that help arrived. And it arrived in such a way that he was forever helped—famous once more, and, once more, his friends came calling and seeking his views on this matter and that, while the woman lay down in her own soil—for she had made it herself and now must stay there.

Today, if you are considering being evil in your intent against someone, first count the cost and ask yourself, "If this goes wrong for me, what's the worst thing that could happen?"

And in this, make sure you count the soil of your own body's stink, for it is this stink that makes you work on this question in the first instance, and this stink inside a person always ends up outside of them as well... should they act in a way that stinks towards someone else.

FOUND!
Once, a little child was so frightened that she cried out to her mother for help. "Mother, I need your help!" she cried, and her mother came at once and soothed her.

"Why are you so frightened?" the mother asked the child. "You have nothing to fear, for I am here and will not let anything happen to you."

The child felt happier and left her mother to be with friends and make witches hats and broomsticks in a playpen. Twice the universe looked inside, and twice the universe saw the child playing without understanding what the game was.

"Frightening times are coming for this child," said the universe. "She has called another power into the wind that also comes swiftly, and now this power has surrounded her in a way

I cannot be close enough to help. I will care for her as much as possible and bring the future in such a way that I will be closer to her than I am today." And this is what happened.

Time was not friendly to the child, who grew into womanhood and sought the love of men, and of farm animals, and friends with peace pipes containing funny matter. Along the way, she found them to all be false and to want her downfall—even the fast furry friends she loved were hard to her, making her suffer with injuries and pain from kicks and bites.

Time looked ahead and saw a place where she could be found once more and planned the days to make sure she was there. And so it was that time changed circumstances, and small molecules switched outcomes and chances and choices to ensure the woman could be at the place where the universe could become more important to her than her broomsticks and magic wands.

Suddenly the day arrived, and the night brought much magic into its being with the woman who, at last, asked the universe for its assistance.

"*I am here,*" answered the molecules, "*and I know everything about you—and I love you.*"

The woman was sincerely surprised at the truth being at last revealed: 'There is a great power! Greater than broomsticks and magic wands, and this is the power of love—love for the world and its people and creatures, and love for those who love it back!'

With this knowledge, the lady made herself beautiful inside and out and became ferociously careful with the ways of the universe so as to please and give back to it.

"At last," said the lady, "I have found the path to happiness and freedom and joy, and will not ever let it go, nor will I ever leave it—for once I was lost, and now I am found."

This day, if you are lost and need finding, consider this tale, for it is a true one, and the truth sets us free.

THE PENALTY

Little money matters started being quite serious money matters, and the worthiness of the one who had them was called into question by others.

"Where is our payment?" they asked. "We worked for you, and you gave us no money, and now we have nothing to take to our children this evening."

The man who had the money matters was sorry for their situation but could not help, for someone had not paid him also. He called his debtor and said, "I need this money today as I cannot pay my own workers," and the debtor said, "I am not in a position to pay as someone has not paid me either."

And so it was that the money kept being delayed and delayed until, in the end, no one got paid—for the wealthiest man had not become wealthy by paying people. Instead, he became wealthy by not paying them, and his family lived in a beautiful house with a beautiful driveway with long-standing trees and fountains and birds that strutted with beautiful plumage that fanned and made green into blue into white and back to green again.

Today, if you want to become wealthy, think upon the cost, for the cost you will bear by not paying your workers is this: you will not have a tremor in your body or a calling on your life; you will not have feelings or heartfelt emotions; and you will not have sincere friends or help when you need it. Instead, you will cause the downing of your own body once it needs to rest from this world, and then you will know there is always a cost.

Fun and laughter may be good for a day, a year, or even a lifetime, but fun and laughter for an eternity is much more generous and much more enjoyable and much more remembered.

And remembered is what you will be—remembered by those who now enjoy their lives and see your own self suffering—for this is the penalty for those who profit from another's misery: darkness... frightening darkness.

REMEMBER THE WORTHY ASPECTS
Lately, the worthy aspects of being in love were not remembered; a writer was being born, and yet the writer had not remembered the loneliness of being alone for many years before her partner arrived.

She worked and worked and worked at her own understandings and made sure they were known to him also. "Forever, you were not this man when I met you," she said, "and you were more understanding of my own needs and wants and desires. But now you are not this man anymore, and I am a fool for thinking this was going to be forever."

"At last," the man said to himself, "I cannot make this lady happy. I have tried and failed, for I was not well in my mind after what had happened, and, now I am, I can make my own way home each night, for now I have work."

So he went to another's home and made his life there, leaving his wife for the one who had reached out and made him happy once more. And they laughed and enjoyed life with one another, for at last the day had arrived for the man when this was possible. Were the lady he really loved to have waited on him more, it would have been her future instead. And, so it was, she wrote about it—for the lady is me.

Remember this, therefore, all ladies with partners who go astray and fall: stand by your man, even when his ways with you are not as you would have them, for this will ensure the future you wish for is yours and not another's who did nothing to get it.

KEEP YOUR MONEY

Small people were talking amongst themselves: "We know she is good, but we don't want anyone else to know, so we will say nothing," and this is what they did.

Time passed, and the horse was ready at last. She had much to give those who walked and rode with her, and her legs went quickly to the line where winners are made.

"So," cried all the viewers, "that horse was the one we'd heard whispers of from all the inside people who said it can win, but why did it win by so much when we could not find any form on our betting sheets?!"

Laughter came from the smallest of the small people: "We had the horse that runs faster than the others, for we hid her among our own friends, and now she is revealed. Wait until you see her next start, for this time we will not hide her in the fields of others but will bring her to the eyes of the world!"

And so it was that the horse hidden from curious eyes made its way into the race that stops the nation. And the race that stops the nation did just that—it stopped—at three o'clock exactly. And all who watched were amazed, as the horse won and paid so much that no one collected a cent—for all the track gallops it had raced in had been foretold to only a few, and only the few knew how good the horse really was!

Beware, therefore, the one who lodges money on a race that so many in the world also bet on, for in this way you may lose it, as the horse that wins may not be the winningest horse before the race. Instead, it may be the horse the smallest of people have hidden from others so no one sees its genius.

Friends of many are good horses, and friends of few are horses that pay so well that even the smallest of cents placed on them makes millions of cents.

Friends, a time will come soon when this horse races. Be sure to know its name when it does, for your own gifts to the bookmakers will instead be payments. And payments are rare in the world of racing over long periods of time, for payments are not made by horses but by small friends of horses—and their friends also.

Look and learn; for this day, your money is your own and is in your pocket. A light therefore to live by, as money is from the light that gives it and should be kept for more important things than winning on horses, which no one can do over a long time.

Written in time is this standard, and, so, you cannot win; only lose. And the day you win is the day you do not gamble.

A friend once said, "This horse is a certainty," and so it won, so others may call theirs certainties also. But a certainty is never a certainty when gems so small are hidden in races and no one sees them. Remember this story the next time you want to bet, and you will keep your money the light has given and live once more in the blessings it brings.

NATURAL IS BEST
Swiftly, whole days flew by, and nights as well. The workers left their jobs for holidays and made themselves happier than they are during the year, when not all the friends and family members are able to be on leave from their jobs also.

One was very happy, for her year had been troubled and difficult and sad—and lonely too—for, while she had people at home, they were also sad and lonely, lost in their thoughts of what had happened.

"Let's do something to celebrate this time," said one to the other. "Let's draw each other as we see our reflections in the mirror." And they did this.

One drew a face so archaic, the other laughed long and hard: "See my wrinkles; they are not that bad. And see my hair; I am not that bald!"

The other had drawn the lady with few wrinkles and much hair and left out his own thoughts of her facial operations, for they were more obvious to him than she knew.

He made her beautiful, and she was pleased, saying to him, "I am beautiful in this drawing, and yet I have wrinkles and not as much hair as this."

He laughed to himself, thinking, 'Well, I had no choice, for I know your vanity with what's in the mirror.'

And so, the game ended with one happier than the other, and no one hurt or called ugly.

If you are vain with what you see in the mirror, remember this fable, for it is not untrue—for operations have much to hide in themselves and can make the operated-on look strange in the mirror. But not strange enough for people who love them to say something, as, in saying something, they may no longer be appreciated and may even be defriended.

Simple living is the best. Simple in its being natural, for natural is what most opposites like, and natural is the best inner and outer beauty of all.

NEW BEGINNING

So long it went on for—so long, the years passed, and much money was spent. Foretold in time were the issues that came—one had a mental problem, another had a serious health issue, and another had both.

"Right," said one, "I am leaving this life today," and he took it, also leaving the possibility of ever being whole on the earth that works to give this to its people.

Another thought, 'If he can do this, should I also try?' and he went mad thinking about it, calling out to people on the street, "What you are is what you are not. Look at this world. It is not made for me, but for all of you who stare!"

A day passed. And another. And another. And the party of three made their own ways in the worlds they now lived in. The one who had left was alone in darkness with no one to guide him home to the light. The ones that stayed made their peace with drugs, and friends that were not friends—but were if drugs were there.

A drug is not a friend to the person who makes it one. Instead, it is a forever lit-down version of quiet exhilaration that becomes a nightmare of hellfire for the one who makes it a friend. The day of its friendship slides into the night of its hell made into life—life that involves finding and hurting and hurting and finding into each single moment.

A drug is that for a reason, for it drugs the being that takes it into a lifemare of nightmares—nightmares that have no end unless ended one way or another.

If on this day you have not yet taken a drug that will do this to your life, do not do it, for you are already whole and can make the world into a better day. If, however, you have done this, remember this folklore, for it is yours to have and hold until the day you choose to end it—one way or another.

Let the ending be one that allows the world to live with you in it as a whole being, and whole you can be if you decide to end it in a good way. Rehabilitation is waiting—a friend forever said so, and this friend is my own self.

A new beginning is waiting for the one who chooses it. Race, therefore, to its door, for the door has a name on it, and it is yours. An odyssey begins and ends here.

LOOK INSIDE YOUR HEART

So long it had been, and now it was here; here and there and there and here; a work made entire was now a work brought into life-giving goodness—for the one who made it happen was the one who can be there and here and here and there.

Over there was a nice person wanting to be nicer, and over here was a person who was not nice and who needed to be nicer.

Truth drifted in the wind and found the nice person wanting to be nicer and helped the lady with her dreams answered and made nicer at last. Caution was required around the other, who was not ready for truth to be known, for the other had lies alive inside their manner of being—lies that made their ways uncertain, for they had lived them for so long, they had become truth to them.

Winds blew, and howls of protestors were made into howls of protest. "This man has told a lie to his wife and his family and to us!" they shouted. "And he has made a mockery of the parliament he sits in. We want him to leave today!"

And so, the man who lied left and was made a fool to the world.

Time passed, and the world realised the man had not lied to them, or to his wife, or to anyone. Instead, the lie had come from the one who needed to be made nicer, for their heart was full of deceit, and they had worked the wind of truth into a howl of lies.

Forever, the wind of truth looked at the one who had made the lie so truthful it was believed by many and thought, 'This person has made my friends unhappy, and it is time now for her life to be made unhappy so she can look for me in her heart—which is where I live and wait for all those who dream of a better day for their lives.'

And this is what happened: the man went to the newspaper and told his story at last, and the woman was made into a gust of wind that carried her lies into the past and made her own self nicer than she could ever have been.

If today you are not someone who is nice and you need to be made nicer, remember that the winds that blow will eventually blow on you, and then you will know what to do. For the day you look inside your own heart is the day you will find the lies that live there blown away by the truth that surpasses all understanding—for it is this truth that you will be made known by.

A cautionary tale, yes, but one that you will remember given time and energy, and all such manners of being will come to pass. It always does.

CHAPTER SEVEN

QUESTIONS AND ANSWERS

FORECASTS

Small slips of fractions passed and turned into larger ones. Fractions of minutes became blocks of time and hours and days and months and years. Decades passed, centuries, and millennia and, still, the earth turned round and round and round, never stopping its orbit around the sun, which burned so brightly that it lit up the days as the world turned and turned and turned.

Forever it turned, never stopping—ever. And no one thought about what makes it turn; they only knew it turned at perfect times each day to make the day a perfectly timed one.

Seasons are not seasons without the turning of the world, and the seasons that shape the world do so in ways that make it continually change. Forever this has been so, and forever it will be so, for the world will keep turning and changing and changing and turning. Humans cannot change this fact. They can only live with it in ways that balance the favours of the seasons to slow the changes rather than speed them up.

If this day you are concerned that the world will not be here for your children or grandchildren or their children, do not be concerned about the world's forecasts, for its forecasts are its own—not those of a human.

Be, however, concerned about human forecasts, for the forecasts of the human beings on this world is a smaller outlook;

their own anger and wrath are what control it, and there are no winners in sincerity for anger and revenge—instead, only forever forgiveness. Find this, and you will find the future for your family and yourself.

A world turns, and so does another, one not far away—one that has your future in it.

THE MANAGED EARTH

Further to the moment when sun days are not actioned, the meadowling went to drink.

'I am thirsty,' thought the animal. 'I have much today that I must do, yet I must drink. And this is how I must be, as I am an animal that has to be near water.'

Afraid, the animal walked close to the water to drink from its well of life.

"Aha," said the crocodile, "a victim I may eat, for I am hungry, and this is my prey coming to greet me."

Too late! ...and the mild creature was made into foretold happy meals and treats for all. The crocodile ate, the friendly beasts that sit on his back also had something good, and the worms in the mud ate also—for they need food such as this as well.

No sooner had they eaten when another meadowling came by to drink. Cautioned by the noise and tastes of a friend now left for the next life, the much-loved creature was forewarned and ran to halt its watered needs for another time, when the crimes against winter were less than the summer.

Much ado was furthered in the pond of murk, where creatures needed their morsels.

"Where is our lunch!" they cried to each other.

'And where are our fetid morsels of love from the sky that

meets us?' they also wondered. 'Justice is swift, and we also need loving cups of tender meats, or we die also!'

'Poor beings,' thought the sun day as it looked on further and further. 'Poor beings of hunger—I love you also and wish no more for your struggles in life.' And so, the day sent another meadowling to the putrid water to drink of its lasting benefits.

"Watch out!" shouted the other. "There are managers in this home of muddy waters that will take you in, and you will not survive!"

Aghast, the worthy animal ran from the edge just in time to leave a disappointment so great that the worthless creatures decided to die. And this is what they did, one by one. The biggest left first, and this left something for the others to taste, and the smallest left last, and this left something for the earth to mature in.

At once, the putrid waters evaporated, and the sun of the day looked upon it with warmness and love at the same time. "I have sent the nourishment this place needed," said the rays of light, "for it needed to move to another place of less harmful sunlight where it will grow and sustain itself better than in this place, which has changed winters and summers."

And this is what happened: the waters sprang up in a new home away from the rays of light and away from the iciness of winters of darkness, and life formed in it and around its boundaries. And, this time, the waters were teaming with good things for the chain of friends and enemies to eat, and, this time, the meadowlings had space to take their chances at life and death.

This is how the sun manages the earth: by always moving things to new places where harvests are plentiful. If this day your home is too hot or cold to sustain you and your lifelong friends, make a new one in a new place where the sun has moved these pictures of health to—for they are always moved to a new place and never are they lost forever—for where an ocean once was, a forest now is, and where a forest once was, a savannah now is.

These are the ways of this world, and while man can harvest much, he may also harvest much across a wide land of plenty, for lands of plenty abound still today. And the lands of poorness are simply waiting for their time to be plentiful once more.

Rest knowing this, for this day, you have plenty in your own backyard and someone else does not. Help them to see the way to a new place, for yours will one day be less than it is now, and you may need the same help.

Refuge is not a frightening thing if managed by those who have this wisdom. It is, instead, a gift from the sun on the day of actuality. Live knowing this truth.

MOTHER EARTH KNOWS

Level crossings roared past the window as the matter was heard.

"If this is the way I am today," said the man to himself, "then how will I act tomorrow? Today, I was down because people are at war with my ways, yet this is how I am. But this challenge is a new one, for I need to be with them, not against them. Today I must make amends and say to everyone that I believe the sun has heated the world so much that humankind is at fault, and I believe humankind can change this."

So he went to the conference and said what everyone else said for the same reason: humankind is at fault for heating the world, and we can stop the heat by being more careful with emissions.

"Right!" said the people who listened and had made the situation. "We are happy now and know our future will be a better, more green one," as this is how they understood and wanted their politicians to be—all agreeing with them to get their votes by not disagreeing.

Yet this is how the politicians got to the top in their professions to begin with: by being smarter than all the others who voted for them—and this was why they were voted for.

Today, a matter is being heard around the world that seeks to bring global warming into man's hands. Yet it is the nature of the world to warm and cool, and warm and cool, and warm and cool, and has been since it started maturing into shape and form so humankind could live on it without concern for many generations.

This day, if you think man can stop the world from warming or cooling, decide who to vote for carefully, for it may not be the cleverest or smartest candidate. Instead, it may be the candidate who agrees with your view—a view with a narrow understanding of a world with more history than you are aware of and more soil underneath your feet than you know—for under your feet is proof that humankind does not cause warming or cooling.

The mother of the earth does this so people can have its goodness for fuel and fire and their nights at home when energy is needed—for the world has energy within it—and the energy you seek that comes from outside is very good at spending the world's energy to make its panels and turbines and rockets of gas.

And one day you will see that the fuel underfoot is less harmful than the waste of metal and gases that surround the homes of your children, who ask, "Why did our parents do this thing?! We have nothing but miles of healthy farms covered with ugly wind turbines that do not rot or rust and work themselves only when they want to, not when we want them to. And the planet now has gas that leaks and causes bad side effects for our health and our children's health.

"We were better off burning natural fuels that trees can grow larger and feast on and making these fuels with less waste and hazards than the solutions made by people who thought they could stop the world from growing warmer in its warm cycles!"

Today, if you are this person, listen to this tale of woe and know it is one, for the tale is just starting—a frightening outcome for the ones who create it for their children.

A saying is this: Policed is this world; policed by Mother Earth, and Mother Earth knows when to warm and cool. And today is time for warming. Leave it be, knowing its lungs will clear the air, for the fuel it burns is the food of the world, without which the world would not exist, for carbon is carbon; carbon is fruit: the fruit of the world and its inhabitants—the fruit of you.

TRUTH, NOT FICTION

Lights were actually arriving, and little helpings of lovely works were being planned for the Earth and its better people, as, for once, they were not at war and no one was being harmed in any way. And the Earth held its breath, as it was not always happy with those on board its ship in the universe of ships with beings on them.

'Well,' thought the Earth, 'here we are, and here are the ones who can help this world of mine. What can I do to say hello? I can cool, or I could heat, or I can stay at a temperature that is one degree higher for the ones who like it that way and one degree lower for those that don't.'

Just at that time in the space continuums, a lighter day arrived—one where the world could think its answer through...

"Surely there is one," said the earthbound inhabitants.

'Surely there is one,' thought the space binary beings.

'Surely there is one,' thought the creatures on both 'toids of finished articles of clothing.

...And there was: "Leave and go to another world, one

where you can make your own choices—for my choice, this day, is to own my own temperature and do as I want to, and that is this: called-for snowbound frozen wastelands for a millennia, then deserts of camels and nothing else for another, the seas risen to heights of skyscrapers then lowered to floors of sandy scrolling white salt, and forests of conifers covering years of worldly plains and grasses with nutrients and fires to burn them into the ground and cover them with woods broken and soiled.

"What will you do while I do these things, if you are here?" the world asked its inhabitants and those on the galactic journey of a lifetime.

"Well," said one, "we could enjoy the ride ourselves, for you are our mother and will not hurt anyone."

'This is so true,' thought the beings on the food-for-free-if-you-can-eat-it voyage. 'We know this as a fact, as our world does the same, and we just call it, *Temperamental, but never trying to hurt us.*'

"Kindly humans, would you like to come and see for yourselves? We have much more history than this world has recorded, so we know this as truth, not fiction, whereas your history of records of weather is only just beginning."

'Well,' thought the earthbound beings, who the planet cared a great deal for: "You are very kind to let us know this, as we can now work with greater understanding than we have this day and moment in our lineages. Why not be as understanding of our Earth when it warms and cools, and also let the excitement of what it will do next be something calming rather than frightening."

And this is what they did: they built snow cone homes and desert tents with water troughs for camels and other kinds of creatures that drink; they made forests with tree huts and little tents for sleeping out in; and for wood, they collected and burned it for the trees to feast on—for trees love carbon, and the more there was, the more they ate and the stronger and taller they grew.

One day, the world had a lot of giant trees. The next, they were thrown into the fire by the world that created them. And the next, they ate the floor of the seas as they rose and fell, with salt covering much of the world that ate this also.

Today the same is happening, and yet no one is calling the world to ask for its plans. If they did, they may find out about the next stage of development—one where more resources are made for its inhabitants to enjoy and make life from.

Little is known right now, but one day it will be. And, one day, you may also know. A writer has written.

MAKE WISDOM YOUR CHOICE

Small, quiet justice was, at last, in the home of the people who had made their friendship with the one who has power. Light had shone on their friends and on their foes alike, but not on them; for the day had been made dark—so dark that they could not be in love with it.

Choices were made, and the one who had the final say made it, "I am withdrawing from being in public life that people look at all the time. It's not my will to be that person anymore."

And this made the lady work hard for many, many, many days and months and years, as he had not considered the implications of starting a new job so late in his later years.

And late it was, for he was late. Late in being at peace with her for measuring him by his wealth before he lost it. Late in his understanding that wise people need to be wise all the time to outwit the world, which always works against the ones who have light in their lives. And late to come to an understanding that he was not always the centre of the world's attention, and he would not always be in their fast calls.

And so it was that the man who had the final say was finally said. Said of this, of that, and of the other. And said in other cautionary ways—but said nonetheless.

He said and said and said and said, and no one heard. Then, at last, someone did! It was a wonderful hour, and he was joyous. "At last!" he said to others. "I knew if I said enough, eventually someone would hear me and listen—for I speak words of wisdom now. I had not these merry ways before, for I had not the wisest upbringing to teach me wisdom, but now I am wise, people hear me."

On this day, if you are not listened to, it is because you are not yet wise and must learn to be wise before those around you will listen. This is the way of this world, and in this world are you.

Today, make wisdom your choice and your calling, for being wise is the greatest thing a man, woman, he, she, or they can be.

Being wise in the world of humankind is sufficient but being wise in the worlds of far places even more so. Bring yourself to this wisdom, and people will want you to speak.

ASK AND YOU WILL BE GIVEN

'The poorness is the soul's forgiving of itself,' thought the man. 'I am poor, and I am forgiven. But the worth of my working hands is still sincerely poor.'

At last, he went to the place he knew to go and asked for help: help to be well in his blessed home; help to be well in himself; and help to be well in the days the called-for, who want help but not to pay for it, request: "Today I am better than yesterday. And today I am worthwhile of being paid."

And that is what happened—he was paid at last!

The invoice said to his money account, "I am here at last, and look, there is more than you asked for, for you asked for this much but have been given this much. We like you and do not wish for you to leave."

And this made the man so happy that he immediately thanked the power for this blessing, for the power was who he had asked for help, and the power had helped straight away—for this is what happens when people ask with a gift of love inside their heart: a trouble is removed, a time of poorness is made shorter, and a gift is sent swiftly.

Ask, and you will be given the same opportunities as those who wait on the power to send. And send He does—always.

THE WAITERS

People are called to live in their *also sweet* life and to be *also sweet* to their family and friends and people they meet, and *also sweet* to their own self: sweet to their inside and to their outside; sweet to their bodies and to their minds.

For the mind has a sweetness... and a sackcloth of worry if the owner wishes to subsist in that clove of garlic; the horrors of the night and the pieces of excrement made up by thoughts of dire consequences that never unfold in the way thought.

Foretold are they to the owner of the clove, who waits in precious time for never-lessons of fate: waiters visit, and waiters call for service in these precise times of sincere sadness. 'Come to me and be a friend,' they say, waiting for you to beckon. "I will be there swiftly if you call," they answer.

Friends are these—if you want them to be. Friends who are enemies of your self-centeredness that places you at the centre of the world's enclosed spaces. "I am the only one who thinks this way," you say to yourself. "I am the only one who thinks I am better than I am and know more than everyone else."

Believe this, and you will meet your waiting friends, who are trouble and fight for your own manner of being. Foretold is this way of personage; foretold is this day of trouble; foretold in the awake time when you are ridden with attitude and despair.

Friend, do not trouble the waiters—for the waiters are the trouble.

THE VOICE OF CALM REASON AND HOPE
"Be at once happy," said the man to the person who was not this way inside, "for if you are not, I will go and never return."

"I cannot," said the man of the homestead of choices. "I need you to know my difficulties and believe in me before I can believe in myself. For today, I have called my waiting friends to get to know me more closely, and they say I am worthless and of no value. Too soon did they want me to posture this way, and too soon I angered them by calling myself worthy. They have decided I must be unworthy, and unworthy I am!"

"Never!" said his friend. "Never believe the voice of discord; the voices of maturity are not those of disinterest and dismay. The voice of maturity is this: you are welcome, you are life, you are made, you are worthy, and you are my friend. Listen to this voice, and you will be made worthy at once."

And this is the day you are, for this is the choice you make: the voices of tuned fire and trouble versed and juxtaposed against the voice of calm reason and foretold hope.

Leave the ones behind that are not this voice and follow only that which is. Do this in memory of the little, sweet, pretty, kind, sincere love inside, for this is your own wisdom, and this is the wisdom of this world—a world made better with your own way within it.

Sweet day, be this day with me that you give me your fruit and your wisdom. And live with me foretold in the knowledge my worries are taken care of already.

Frightened no more.

WAIT UPON INVIGORATION

Small hurts were recollected, and the more they were recollected, the more they hurt. Heartfelt apologies were made, and yet, small hurts were still not forgotten.

The man was hungry, and so was his wife—hungry for likeable friends and likeable financial blessings, yet where were they this day when the vehicle was going? Where were they this day when it stopped to share a meal? And where were the mandates that bring frozen solitude to life?

Time passed...

At once, the man was happy; at once, the lady was also, for at once, the mandates arrived.

"Go to this house and make this way clear," the Father had said to his Son. "Make the bettered home into a happy one also, and at once joyful."

And so it went foretold: a foretelling of wealthier moments and happier friends and changed beings—for beings need hope to help their days of adversarial choices turn into wholeness. And wholeness needs their choices to be fretful without being frightening.

Choices are that which make this world what it is. And choices can be guided or be driven, but not ever can they be pretended, for once a choice is made, its consequences are known. And these are those fearless beds that come in the night to haunt and heckle, should the choice be a bad one.

Make your choices carefully, and you will sleep well. Make them carelessly, and you will get what you will for: a fright in the night, a fear in the day, and a level crossing that comes too quickly to manage.

Chase your dreams and be at peace with your

considerations, knowing the power will invigorate you at the time you need invigoration, for this is what occurs: invigoration without knowledge of understanding why—just knowledge of *must action* and *must respond*.

A financial blessing if you do this choice machine a favour and wait upon invigoration. A salient outcome is here—financially, a blessing!

THE ANSWERS
"Why is it that every time I want something to go my way, it goes the other way?!" exclaimed the woman, who had many things go her way and, yes, some that didn't—some that may have changed her life for the better and some that may not have too.

"Every time I want something, it goes to the some-matter place where I can't get at it, for that place is not my place ever—that place is where other people have gifts, for they are lucky, and I am not. My luck is not ever with me. It is some-matter that goes somewhere else, and to someone else who does not deserve it as much as I do!"

And so she ranted in cross, tense words that made her feel better about her luck not being there.

Long winds blew and came to find her in time. They knew her well, as they had often passed by, wanting to give her dreams into her hands but not able to, for she was not ready in so many ways. She had a bad attitude towards some things but not others, and she was incorrect in thinking some ways but not others. And was often so close to being blown with good fortune that some days it came and some days it did not, but most often, it passed by on its way somewhere else.

One day the winds were coming with a gift for her, and she refused it, for she said, "I do not want this role at work. It is not my role but someone else's to have, and I will let them have it, for surely, it is not the winds that have brought this to me but the friends who made it available. And the winds are not bringing this as a gift to me, but as a test." And so she missed out.

Another time, the winds brought her a new house to live in, and she loved it so much that she gave it a name. Yet she told the sky she had no luck in her life, so the winds were unable to bring payments for it as much as they tried to.

And sometimes her words made the winds blow elsewhere, for they were not right in their ways towards others.

And, so it was, the lady was not ever really lucky—just blessed in other ways that made sure she had a house and a vehicle to keep warm in on wet or windy cold days, and friends who made visits and shared wine and laughter.

Time passed, and the winds found the lady willing to be better in her thinking, and more generous in her gifts to others who needed financial and kind assistance, and with more of their own ways in her—so much so, she made herself shine with light from inside to outside.

The light was strong, and the winds found it awesomely powerful—so powerful, the winds came and brought cattle and finds of geldings and mares to her home as a gift from the stars to make her soul delight in that which it already delighted in.

Friends were quickly on the scene to share in the happiness—for friends are always found when someone's wealth increases so much that they become healthy financially and have more to give in the way of lovely lunches and long breaks on holiday. And, sometimes, the lady remembered her complaints and saw her duality in wanting more when she was not quite right in the ways of the universe.

"I am sorry," she said to her heavens above. "I am sorry that

I was not correct in saying to you more often that I am sorry. I know you saw me and wanted more for me, and I was not ready. And I thank you that you see me now and say I am, for this day, I have much to share with the people of the world and the neighbours in my street— who were always there and looked at and learned from me in my social posts.

"And now that you have shown them that I was just waiting for your arrival, how can I be of greater help to the world, now that I am this blessed?"

The stars looked upon her, thought for a moment, and said, "Say this to the earth: *Look at the book I wrote for you and give it your efforts to understand, for the day when you do, is the day you will also be blessed. And in being blessed, you will also be ready for the winds that blow favour on your lives and your families, and you will know that, sometimes, it is good to be without as much as you want. For the ones who have much will always want more, and the ones who do not will seek the answers to life, the universe, and all in it.*

"*This is the gift to all, and it is this gift that the winds of time gives to you. Freezing sometimes, yes... Difficult sometimes, yes. Wonderful sometimes, yes... And, in the end, blessed, as, in blessing, you are brought to life.*"

Read and learn, all those who open these wise tales of lives lived and bring the understandings to your souls, for today, the lady has won her blessing, and you can share in the prize—the prize of wonders, joys, and blessed lives. Forever, it is so.

A wind comes this day to blow on you—listen, for it is already here.

A LESSON LEARNED

Lifting herself up was oh, so hard. "It is a good day today," said the woman who had done this thing, "for, this day, I will raise myself to the ceiling of happiness, not the floorboards of gloom. I will spend the day on me, walking and shopping and not working—for it's Saturday and today I am free of the week and my work and my hardships in going there and being a worker who is very good."

So this is what she did: she went shopping and saw beautiful things she liked and wanted to buy.

Her purse was not as happy. "I am empty," it said. "I have no money to work today, and yet you keep buying these things on after-payments that I don't see in the future. How are we going to live together if you ignore me?"

Still, the lady looked and saw and bought her way through the day—shoes, a handbag, a dress, and a coat all went out of the purse with no money. The surest thing was going to happen at some point: the lady would not be able to pay for her buyings and, instead, would need to take a loan to cover them.

And this is what happened: the loan came. And then another. And another. And soon, the lady could get no more loans as all her money was spent paying loans that had no end in sight.

She said to herself, "I will bet on horses and pay my loans this way," and so she did, betting large amounts of rent and groceries on them. And, for a time, she worked it well, always winning something, no matter how little—because she concentrated.

Goodness came into her life when she met someone who had a lot of money and who gave it to her to help with her loans. They saw each other and went shopping, buying much in a day. The lady was so happy—for her home was filled with things again! And their love of money was there for all to see, as they had very interesting conversations with one another when the sales went through.

"This will look wonderful near that."

"That will be good with this."

"You will look great with this on."

"And you will look stunning with that around your wrist."

And so, they loved life. And the one who paid the loans started to breathe once more. She said to her purse, "You see, it has worked out. You are nearly full now, and you don't have to be worried anymore."

The purse was hopeful but said nothing, as it was still empty.

Foretold was the day the man fell. And foretold was the day the lady's loans came once more to be a burden. And foretold was the day the purse said, "I was always worried this day would happen, and now it has."

If today you are someone who likes to buy things without agreement from your wallet or purse, remember this lady who is still paying her loans and waiting for her horse to win—for this day is that day.

And today her horse has made its peace with her purse, for today, at last, the universe has smiled on her, knowing she will not ever again make the mistake of buying things without payment for them—a lesson learned the hard way.

SAVINGS OF MUCH

"Buy now—I have a little sincere need. And buy now—I have a larger one. And buy now—I have a larger one still. And buy now—I have the largest one I could possibly have!" And so the twilighted man bought; he bought to please others and to please himself. And, in pleasing himself, he pleased the live long ability he had willed to himself many years past.

One day, he looked in his wallet, and it was no more—no more ability, no more accusations of wealthier days, and no more trialled social posts.

"Well," said the man, "this is it. I cannot go on, for I bought when I should have saved, and saved what I should not have, which has now been made into trouble for myself. And the diamonds I own must now be sold."

And this is what happened: sold, sold, sold, until all was sold—and for much less than was paid for.

"Why did I not save more in times of plenty and spend less on material things and wonderful activities?" horse-rasped the man who had lost everything. 'Why was I not alone in that way when others wanted my generosity, and I gifted it to them?' he thought. 'Where are they now that I am poor, without friends or family to help me?' And he called himself a fool for not saving more when he had the ability to.

A poor person is never a poor enough person when this happens, for they make themselves poorer in the knowledge of their centred wasting: "Oh, woe is me; I am lost to time, and no man listens anymore. I have foretold my own demise and not done as I should. Where are my social media friends now that I have no life to show anyone? And where are my video posts now that the things on my table are bald and bare?"

One day, this suffering man lay down and did not rise again. He went to heaven and found much to make posts about: frightening lightning, great crashes of light, wonderful meals of perfumed matter that no one knew but all loved to dine on, and written lifted dwellings of beauty such as never seen on earth.

'Well,' thought the man, 'while I lost much on the ground of that world, I have gained all and even more in this world. I did not know I had made many friends so blessed in their lives that I have earned these things. And now that I have them, I will never lose them, for I did have savings—savings of much in the next life.'

And this is how it wisely works for those who gift much to others without care for themselves. Friends are here. Make them your future today.

THE GREATEST JOKE

Funny people said to one another, "This is the joke of the decade! How amusing is this?! People will say we have made this joke into the best one ever told, for it has an ending no one will guess and a fruitful way of saying what it is without being unkind to another person—yet all will know who we speak of," and they laughed and laughed to themselves.

A little boy looked at the joke and said, "This is not my kind of joke, for it has no laughter in it—only sadness, for it is about me."

A grown man looked at the joke and said, "It is about me, and I do not find it amusing."

A lady read the joke and said to herself, "This joke is about me, and I do not think it is funny."

And another person read it and said to their heart, "This is a joke about me, and I do not think it is funny at all!"

And so the joke was not funny to most people who saw it; instead, it was the opposite, for they all thought it was about themselves. And the people who made the assumption it was a joke about the reputation of a certain man were made into fools themselves, for they did not see their own morals of poor standards—for the man they had made into the joke was not even concerned about it.

He said, "If this joke is about me, then I am an interesting person with a life who has lived. And so be it, for in not living life to its fullest, I would not really be alive. And now, if this joke is about me, it is another thing to add to my collection of life stories I will tell in the next life."

And so it was that the joke was not a joke on the man whose

reputation had been sullied with false accusations, but a joke on all those who read it and thought it was about themselves, for they had also made their mistakes—and that is the joke.

To the one who has not made any in their life, your mistake will come also, for all make them. And to think you will not is a joke—perhaps the greatest joke of all.

CHAPTER EIGHT

BELIEVE AND SUCCEED

WORK THEREFORE
Very small people were happy in their world of the racetrack with the animals they love so much. Day after day, they met and worked and dreamed of the day a champion would come to greet them. Since this is rare in their world, they knew it may take a long time, but if they tried, it would come, and so they tried and tried and tried and tried. And they worked and enjoyed their days of dreaming and seeing the sunrise over grandstands and horses with steam in their nostrils.

Forever they worked, and forever they dreamed. Lives passed, and so did horses and grandstands that changed in shape and size. The world also changed and made robots to do their jobs. These beings were intelligent and also started to dream of having a champion in their world, and so they worked and worked and worked and dreamed of fast horses and fast everything, for the world had become fast—so fast, no one could keep up.

Robots took over jobs and cars and horse farms and grew food and made articles for humans, who waited for rain to come on their lives so their lives could be made richer with dreams of fast horses.

Today, if you work hard and have something to dream of, you are richer than they are, for their dreams were lost to leisure, and there are no dreams in leisure—only long days of solitude and happier children but unhappier parents.

Work, therefore, for dreams have joys that are many, even sunrises over grandstands with happy horses and people seeing their lives as one. Dozens of roses cannot change this matter of happenstance, only work.

WHAT MAY BE

Sunset arrived, and it drew the wonders of the world in the sky and lit the earth with its beautiful twists, and people were at once delighted in the treat made for their eyes.

"Look at this," said one, "and look at that also. See the colours and the way they break over the mountains and down the slopes to the sea—it is so beautiful; I cannot see anything in the world as beautiful as this."

"Aah," said another, "I see it also, but I also see the mists of the morning when I wake early, and the sunrise over the lake where I live, and how it brightens the water into bluenesses and purples of just wonderous amazement."

"I know this view also," said yet another, "and also like to see it. But my life sees the blackness of the night where I work at the coal factory, when the stars of many light the blackness so purple, the galaxies seem to be closer than they are. The moon also brightens and fades and is sometimes so big and bold that its beauty is actioned along with the day—for the night also has its amazements."

"Yes," agreed the lady, who also puzzled at the stars, wondering if life teamed upon them or near them. "I see the cosmos also in the books I read and the stories I see on television. The purples and the lights of many colours are so incredible that I wonder at what they do and how they live—for surely, there is life there also?

"Alone in the universe is not how the universe was made, for life is everywhere, even on barren bottomless oceans with hot volcanoes and vents that steam life around them. Surely the same goes in the heavens above, where impossible possibilities are possible and possible possibilities unfold!

"Surely the days and nights there are the same as here, where beings look upwards and wonder about us. Surely, they know we are also in wonder at their ways and knowledge and pleasures and flights of fantasy."

For this is how workers are: workers who work to be at once thoughtful of others, thoughtful of possibilities, and thoughtful of what may be—for what may be is that we are not alone, and what may be is that we were never alone—for the Earth has attractions such as those of faraway places we want to visit and travel to. And, in this way, we look and see and experience just as others do—and just as the ones that live on spacetime continuums may also do.

For space is time, and space has time to travel and visit faraway places. And sustenance is needed on these travels, as is the power they need to be what they want to be—and these things sometimes require the twilight to find. And the twilight is when you will see the visitors who wave and wish to say hello one day.

Be nice when they do, for they have been nice to you by not interfering with your culture and your universe of amazements, for amazed they are that you are here on this pined-for block of crystal justice for all—a justice they want the world to have, and yet, it seeks to be at war.

Friends are here. Be one as well.

ATTUNE YOURSELF

Soon the day went away, and the night fell. Always the night falls, and when it does, the people cry with relief: "We made it to another day! We went out and worked all day looking for wheat and materials to build our homes, and we foraged for scraps and leftovers—and, today, we made it, for night has fallen and we are alive still!"

The night looked over these people and said to itself,

"Tomorrow is another day—a day when you may not work, for the day has wind and rain and heat so searing, your cries for water will not be heard."

And this is what happened when the day arrived: the rain fell so hard that the ground covered the scraps and the wheat could not be culled; the wind blew so hard that the people could not stand in it, let alone walk or work the soil they needed to till; and the sun scorched the ground and made it so hot that the hands of the workers burned red and blistered, sending them to shelter—for shade was the only thing they needed.

And the day made itself clear to those with no wealth in their countries like the others had: "You are not worth my day today. You are not worth my light or my houses of wealth. You are worth nothing to anyone except yourselves, for you have not made wealthy houses or jobs or cars or streets to drive on. You have only made scorched earth muddy, and muddy earth scorched. You have made nothing with the millennia given to your people to make good things from. Instead, you have chosen to live as you do, and this is your own fault."

The workers sat and looked at the day and heard its mockery of their lot in life, and they laid down and decided not to be concerned about the next time the day attended their homes and their days—for that day, they died and were lifted through the night to the eternal spring waiting for them.

At last, they were given houses and food and life in all its happiness and healthiness, and so they looked at their lives on earth and said, "It was worth it, for without that struggle, we would not have asked the light for help, and the light has done this for us."

And they looked at those who came to meet the light but were not able to enter its doorway, for they had not looked for it on earth or asked for its help, and were sent to the darkness, which opened its arms and welcomed them into it—forever dark and black and cold and grey and without happiness or sincerity.

And the ones who had suffered in life agreed, saying, "We were cared for, as we made friends with the light that visited our doors when we needed it to."

And so it was that the happiest were unhappy in their life on the Earth, and the happiest on Earth were unhappy with their life in the world to come. Attune yourself to this, and you will meet the light on your journey after this world is ended with you, and you will also be most fortunate to have the light greet you and take you into it.

A tale this is—yes—yet in your heart, you know it to be true. Search, therefore, and know that in searching, you will find the truth—for this book is for seekers of truth, and this is the truth you seek.

TRUE TO YOURSELF

People went to the fair and had a wonderful time! It had berry ice cream and fruit-flavoured ice, and magnets with stickers that made people smile. It had floss and dogs that were hot and fierce lions, and free entry into markets and swings and scary rides.

It had everything anyone could possibly want to do at the fair, and so everyone was very happy... except the beasts, who wanted to go back to their farms and rest in the shade of a tree, away from all the noise and running children and people who looked at them and judged them unworthy of a prize.

Those who had won prizes were not so indifferent, for they were crowing their own praises to the others who had not.

"Look," one said, "my prize is bigger than yours, for my prize has many colours and its size is larger—this must mean I am better than you are."

Another said to the bull, "You are mistaken, for the more colours there are, the less you are. You must have one colour, and that is blue—for mine are all blue, and that means I am better than you."

So, they disagreed with each other.

"My prize is better."

"No—my prize is better!"

And this went back and forth all day at each other.

The night-time came, and their carers returned to their prized bulls. One was not as happy as the other, saying to herself, "This bull has won much, yes, but I wanted to be blue all the way through." The other said to himself, "My bull is the *Best in Show*, and I am very happy for now I can make more bulls like him and extend my life's actions and options."

And so it was that the farmers went back to their properties and each planned for the next fair. One said, "I will send my prize bull to the prize female, and they will have a prize calf," and this is what they did. The other said, "I will let my prize bull rest with my herd and make them stronger," and this is what he did.

And so it was that the calves were born. One stood out from all the others—a bull who would be a prize one. It was standing with its mother, who looked at the farmer and said, "Here he is— the son you wanted. I have given him to you, as you chose his father with wisdom helping you."

The man looked at the calf on the other side of the fence from his own and said, "There is the son I wanted. The bull of my dreams is now the bull of the lady who lives next to me. I should have asked myself to explore most carefully the options I had, for I did not, being too confident knowing my own herd was prized. And look, she has outwitted me this year.

"I will do what she did next year and get the bull I want most dearly in my heart, for the one I have grows older and weaker then, and I will need it."

And so, the story went on year after year. Year after year, the two neighbours working to outdo one another, and the prize bulls working the same way at the fairs they went to.

"My colours are better than yours."

"No—mine are better than yours!"

And so on until, one day, a friend came by and looked at the ribbons in both homes and said, "You have the same as each other. I have been to her house, and she has the same ribbons as these."

"Exactly the same?" asked the man.

"Yes," said the friend, "exactly the same," and he asked the man, "Why have you not worked together yet? You could ensure each other's herds are the best in the world with ribbons such as these."

The man answered, "Because my ribbons are better than hers—mine are alright for what I want them for, and hers are alright for what she wants them for."

"I understand now," said the friend. "You are not wanting the best herd in the world. You only want the best herd you can own and control. Your colours are not red, or blue, or green, or pink, or yellow—your colours are *true to yourself*."

And that is what is the ending of this story. It has no right or wrong, no wishes or dreams not coming true, no truth to share, and no moral to tell. Instead, it is about being true to your colours—the ones the light has given you to share with the world—for the world needs you, for only you can make the herd you have better than it is already.

TIME

Time went to bed and woke feeling like it needed time—time to sleep, time to rest, and time to be kind to itself.

Time was always busy, running here and there and making time for other people. And time was not so kind, for time had a way about it that was finite.

Time was always saying, "It's time—it's time you had more work to do, and time you had more friends to meet, and time you had children, and time you had more time for your parents, who raised you in their time."

Time was very demanding and wanted more time from everyone else.

Soon, it was time—time to get up and make time for all the times other people wanted from time.

Time looked at its watch and called to its friends and family, "I have time for you now. I do not have time for you later, or in the morning, for I have this time now but no other time then, as today I have time for you at four o'clock and time for you at ten a.m., but later I need to have time for myself to be on time for this meeting at three p.m. I also want time for my visit to the shops at twelve." And so, time was busy eating itself up in space and time, making time for others and time for itself.

It worked overtime sometimes and made this time up by working less at other times. The clock ticked and ticked as time worked itself through time and space. It made friends with its understandings of itself and made itself known to everyone else as they needed it—some more than others.

Working and living and breathing always takes time, and time was happy about this, for time was its own master—always running out on people, always being a friend then an enemy, always caring and loving... until the last minute. And the last minute was always the one that time liked to be there for—for, at the last minute, people looked in its face and said, "It is finally time, and now this time has ended."

The day is now when you need your time to live inside of it. Think of this day as time you have only once, and you will understand time far more than you do now—for today, it may be your time also.

Remember, time only stands still for those that have none,

and make the most of each day—for time is a friend until it is an enemy. Time runs away quickly and never returns.

THINGS

"Sold!" said the family. "The household is sold. We will go to a new home and take all with us, and we love it so much, we will pay well for it."

The man thought, 'I love my possessions and want to keep them, but at this time, it is the right action,' and so he said, "Sold" as well.

'Sold are my things—my beautiful things I so carefully chose for my home in the city, which is no longer my home. When I bought them, they made me happy, for I was free then, and now I am no longer free. I am with my beautiful woman, who I love and want to live with in the country, but I am no longer free anymore.'

The sadness made him feel even more sad, for his way in the world had been brought to its knees with loss and a casual friend's betrayal.

"How can I ever overcome this?" he said to himself. "I have nothing for my own, and no self-esteem. The woman I met in the darkness has made my newsworthy life a misery, and now everything is sold—even my self-esteem."

One day the man looked back on this day and said to his heart, "It was a day when I lost everything but gained much, for that day, I had the money I needed and the soul food I needed. And the money made a change in my life, for I started to be my own man once more."

And he worked on this understanding and made a promise to himself: if ever he bought things for his home, he would always think, 'These are just *things*. Things I like, yes, but just things. And the money I get for them is better than not having the money I need—for things can be bought again and, next time, I will buy better things. For things are just *things* and cannot replace money when needed, and things are not important to those who need money.'

Money has a way of leaving and returning—and return it will. If you want money, look at your things and say goodbye to them, for things are nothing compared to having your immediate needs met. And immediate needs are these: fridges and freezers with good food in them; a roof over your head, whatever it may be; and a friend to help you through difficult times. And it is the friend who is most important of all, for the friend will see you through.

If you want a friend such as this, ask the heavens, and they will send one, for one is always sent—a friend for the day, a friend for the time, a friend to see you through, and a friend to give you *things*.

RAINY DAYS

The little animal slept. She had been asleep all night and most of the morning, and now it was time to go outside and meet the day.

The day was wet, and she said to it, "Must you be like this today? I would prefer to walk with my mother, for I have not walked with her for some time now, and I would like to spend time with her and her alone."

The day looked at the square black animal and said, "I must be like this, for otherwise, your walk would not be as nice, for in being like this, I water the soil and make everything grow. Without this day, your day would not be nice at all."

The dog thought about this and said to the day, "I am happier now and will play in the dry places and sleep more, for sleep is easy when I do not do anything other than sleep. Sleep is sleepier somehow, and I fall into it so easily; I like being that way—dreaming of rabbits and frogs and all manner of beings I can chase and be friendly to. They are almost as exciting as walking with my mum, only not as good as that—for she is my friend and my master and wants us to sit and stand and be her children."

The day looked at the mother and said to her, "Your time is managed by me, for I am also time. If you want time to walk and be fit and spend time with your dog, you must hurry, for writing on a laptop does not do these things for you. Instead, it eats time and leaves no time for the pet."

The mother looked at the day in the window and said in her own being, "I know you are right, and I want to walk my pet also, for she is my beautiful animal that makes my heart sing, and I know we will enjoy ourselves in this time we have together."

And this is what she did. They walked and looked and talked to the sky and said to the rain, "Thank you." And, so it was; the wet day passed by, and still, everyone made the most of it.

Rain does not harm a walker or an animal. Instead, it gives them joy knowing that once the rain finishes, the sun will come, and so will the hay and the lawn and the grass, and the trees and flowers—for a rainy day is a good day, and there is no other way to think of it, even if you are a dog.

FIND EACH OTHER

Winter arrived, and so did the night—darker than it had been, darker than the day of winter-like homelessness.

The small animal shivered. "I am not at home anymore. I am lost and cannot find my way back. My parents have gone to different homes and left me alone in my bed without anyone to bring me treats and rubbery toys."

Calling for them, the small black friend walked and walked in the days and the nights.

"Where are you, my mother?

"Where are you, my mother?

"Where are you, my mother?

"Where are you that you have left me alone without shelter or a bed to live in as I used to? Where are my clothes and my funny friends? Where is my lasting, beautiful father, who wanted me but could not take me? Why has he abandoned me also—does he not love me anymore? I am lost. Help me!" cried the black chosen one.

At last, a man called to the home that no longer had people. "There you are," he said. "I'm late and could not come sooner, but I'm here now and you are okay, so this is what matters."

The man took the lost dog to the home of his missing parents, who had found each other alone and made their lives together once more.

The pet was frightened at first, saying, "Are you my loved ones—are you really? How could you have missed me in the darkness when you left, for I saw you and howled to the cars as they left? Why did you not return for me?!"

Burnt by their hurried bent excursion, the small furry life lay down and slept and slept and slept.

When it woke up, it felt much better: "I am home once more, and I have this to say to those who are lost: be at once happy when you are found, for being found is better than being lost. Being found is the best action of all, for today I am found, and my parents are with one another, and that is all I need."

Like a child. Like everyone.

JUST A FACE

So it was that the lady went to be a better one at a make-place where they make ladies feel better. In went the needle, and in went the fat, and in went the money to pay for the day of luxury.

'I am much better now,' thought the lady. 'I have my lines straightened and my creases ironed, and I feel like I am much younger again. Today I will make sure I have this paid, for in the past I have not and, instead, placed it in the future payments tray of my wallet. From this, it's clear that they are not paid for—for my credit went out the window, and I was made poor for a long time without the ability to get the needles I want so much.'

Time passed, and again the lady found money from her horse that won races, and again she paid for her needles. And again, and again—and this made her very happy, as her face was her vision in the mirror; a day was not a day when vanity was not there. After all, who would care for her beauty if she did not?

And so, time passed again until, one day, the needles could no longer do their magic for her to see, and the cost was as much as her own car!

She considered this and suffered from it: 'I am ageing and have lost my looks. There is no one who sees me as I used to be, for I am ageing so much that I do not see myself anymore.'

And she lost her feelings towards her face: 'I do not like this and wish for an operation to cure the sagging and bagging.'

And this is what happened again and again, and then, one day, she was considering her mirror and wondered where she had gone to?

"I look funny," she said to herself. "My hair is nicer than before, for I do not put colour on it, and the light I shine there makes it work better at follicle level. But my face is gaunt and has no life in it. I cannot move this or that, and when I smile, my skin breaks this muscle and that one. I feint across the eyes that make flutterings my own heart cannot understand, for my face has a will of its own. What have I done?!"

And so it was that the lady who loved her face so much ended up not loving it any longer and wishing she had not to begin with.

For her face was just a face; it told people she was a good

person, one with friendly features and a smile that said, "I will not hurt you ever," and one that gave people friendly helpings of laughter and happiness.

It was not a machine to create into something it was not intended to be. Instead, it was just some flesh wanting to make friends, and in making friends, it knew it could do this forever if left alone. And by leaving it alone, the lady who owned it could have made a friend of it also.

POISE AND CHARISMA

A troubled man looked at his girlfriend and decided she could no longer be a friend to him. He was caused for in his concern at her facial expressions.

"Are you unhappy with me?" he asked.

"No. Why do you ask?" his girlfriend said.

"Your nose has a wrinkled-up expression, yet the rest of your face does not, and this makes you look disgusted."

"I am," she said. "I am disgusted that my nose will not straighten as the rest has and will get it fixed in the morning," and this is what she did, asking her surgeon for a new expression.

The surgeon asked the lady, "Why do you want this?"

The lady said, "My manager said I look disgusted and wants to know why."

"But your manager is not you," said the lady who fixes faces for a living. "Your manager is only a person with their own expressions. Why do you care so much?"

The caution was now becoming obvious to the lady, who wanted yet another surgical procedure, and she considered her careful plans for another operation: "I asked him to come with me to my room, and he did not, and I feel he would have had my nose been better."

"I see," said the operator. "You are feeling internally unhappy and want to make it external, for in making it external, you can solve the internal unhappiness."

"This is exactly correct," said the patient. "This will make me happy!"

And so, the operation was scheduled for the next day.

The lady hurriedly prepared and made her way to the theatre. 'I am so happy,' she thought. 'I will be perfect in the morning, and then the man will be my homecoming one, and I will be more actively assured than I am now.'

The day was over, and the night came. The lady unveiled her nose and saw that it had no wrinkles anymore. She was so elated that she called the man and said, "Look, I have no matter with my nose anymore."

The man laughed and said to her, "Your nose? You never had a matter with your nose. It is your face that has the matter for me, as I am not attracted to women with house-sized lips and falsifications everywhere.

"I want a natural lady—one with poise and charisma. And this is her standing with me now—the widower from next door who I got to know slowly and who cared for me with meals and laughter and made my day when I saw her; a friend who became a lover. Call me as one, but know, I am not to be your boyfriend anymore."

The lady was shocked: "But I have made myself into what I thought you wanted! For I see men look at women with long hair and large busts and lips."

The man again laughed and said, "Aah yes, we do, don't we? But not to marry. Why would we want a lady who is like that for our children when our children mean more to us than anyone in the world? No, we want a mother for them who is like our own. Fine and upstanding, friendly and loving, caring and caressing.

She is the one we want. The others we do not—except to make love to."

And so it was that the lady, who spent so much time making herself into one of these ladies, learned she should have waited and waited for the man the light would send—for this is the way of the light to do: to send at the time when sending is right and not before. And not to ladies with heavenly masked crusaders inside of their hearts—for their hearts have not remembered to love themselves first.

THE WINNER'S GATE
The one who had her own funny way of being was now happy. She had looked at many other ways of being in the world and chosen the one that was most familiar—her own family's way: the way of horse racing. And she decided that it was no longer for adults only, but also for children with dreams of winning races.

The child grew to become a lady, and she looked at her life as it unfolded and found it disappointing. Nothing ever went to plan, nothing ever was as it could be, and nothing was ever as wonderful as it could be.

She fell into a depression and made mistakes along the way. The ways she chose were not at all wise, and she found herself in the company of people who did not care for her or her needs. Instead, they had their own ways and made her pay for them—a bet here and a bet there, and many bets here and many bets there.

One day, she went to the country to live and find a life without betting. She chose to live on a street with beautiful houses and built one there also. It was a good day when she moved into it and made new friends with her neighbours, who did not bet but wanted to know her as herself.

Today, this lady has a horse running that she owns, and it

has a name—a name like a beating heart that wishes to win for prize money, not betting money. And so it did—winning by a good winning break over its opposition. And now the lady is at peace, for her wonderful day has arrived at last—the day when her horse wins and her matter of writing is complete—for that day is today.

A writer has finished her book. Sincere apologies if you are one who does not care for it. But should you be one who does, then you too can have your day like today, for today the light has shone and the wind has brought blessings from the universe of love. And you too can have these if you listen for the wind to speak to your heart and look for the light to bring you the help you need.

A forever quintessential way and a listen is how it starts. Written into time—a gateway for you to find and walk through. Hallelujah!

THE TRUTH IS HERE

Listen and learn, all those who read these marriages of tales in the book of life, for they are truths you need to live by. Forever they have been so, and forever they will be.

A grateful heart is one that learns from the one that teaches, and the one that teaches has learned these lessons over millennia.

Truths are never not truths, and so it is that, should you apply them, you will know the truth: give and it is given; listen and you will be heard; fear not and you will have nothing to fear—forever, it is so.

Find these truths in the sky above and earth below and in your hearts, and you will know that the truth is there and has much to give—for the truth will set you free forever.

Extra Cautionary Tales
for Serious Seekers of Truth

CHAPTER NINE

CAUSE AND EFFECT

BE NOT ONE
The whole day long, the man was always being witty with people on the box of tricks in his hands. The fool was never any better than the ones whose lives he made quicker with bullied fairy tales, and he was not ever whole in the ways of his own living. Hoping to cause others the same lot in life, he made them think upon his false quips and very underhanded pains.

"I am the one who is here to make your life suffer," he said. "You are not worthy of having life, for you are nice; it's true, but you are fallen because I say you are!"

Too soon the polling booths came, and too soon the man lost all. "You are a troll," said the managed social media account. "You may not say anything anymore about anyone or anything, for, anyway, you are nothing to any one of us who say you are nothing," and the man's life was lost to cut options of nothingness.

Foretold is this way if you choose online bullying tacitness: your acid ways will be returned to you ten, eleven, or ninety-nine times over, for you are nothing and nothing you will be.

Be not one of these—ask, and you can be much more. Find your lived life, and you will find your lost self—a friend said so.

TAME THEY WILL BE
Many children had much to say to the child of difference: "You are sold to this way and have no callings in life. You would be

better off dead, and you have not a skerrick of happiness within you, for we say you are different, and this is what you are—different!"

More and more they taunted, and more and more the child turned into himself and feared the future.

'If I am this way, as they say, what will become of me as I grow up? Who can love me, and who will care for me as I age? And how will I earn enough to pay my way into the future when my dreams are so large?' the boy thought. 'How can this be so when all I need is someone to believe in me, for I believe in myself—so much so, I want to go to Mars and see the stars in space that shine into my room at night, for they are what fascinate me!'

So he looked and looked at the stars and dreamed of what they might be made of and how long it would be in his life before he could arrive on the reddest of them all?

Too soon, the day came when others said to him, "You are not our kind; you are different. Your manner is still, and your words do not console, and you look at others as if we are not here. You are different, and we think you are mad in some way."

And, still, the boy called himself sane and in charge of his own starry nights and sweated days on a computer.

And still, his friendly housemate was not convinced. "You do not seem to be here sometimes," the man said to the man who had grown. "You wish for these things that are not possible and live this dream that has no chance of ever being made true in our lifetimes. And this is your choice, for you are cold towards others and have this way about yourself that is odd to us. We see a man who has hope, yes, but also one who does not. Give yourself some rest and choose to live in the world of went-worth helpers who help the brighter ones to a better day."

"Not I!" cried the child inside the man. "I have much to do and know my hopes and dreams, for one day I will go to Mars!"

And so, he worked and had his monies increase so much that

he became the wealthiest man in the homes of those who watched on television. And they wished they were him—tall, handsome, clever, and wealthy—cleverer than they are and different in ways they have not ever seen.

"What a hope this man is!" they all said.

"What a vibrant help to the world of tomorrow!" others said.

"And what a changed person than the one we knew at schools," said those who had. "Why, he is stranger than us, yes, and he has ways that will themselves onto others who do not, but he has made his funny self into a wondrous self without changing anything. We were not right in what we said to him and what we did."

'Will he be our friend now?' they all wondered.

And so it was that the foreman of himself was now the foreman of those who had made his inner child cry at night, alone in his bed that the maker's sky looked upon.

The maker went to the child and said, "I made this man to be someone in this world who will make a change for the better to it, and you are my carefully wrought foreman who has this quitter inside who knows better than to quit. I know you as I made you, and you are fearfully made to be a challenge to those who are less fearless.

"Be with them now, and know that this day will not last, for soon you will see why your helpless financial situation is now helped and your knowledge of space made into fresh starts and willed aspirations. Tame are they that have you now, and tame they will be, for I have made you as a fresher being with fine detail and finer machinations—for this is what you need to be our star man for the ages: Asperger's."

FINELY THREADED

For all her days, she wanted to be a man—always, always, always. She looked so beautiful that no one ever knew her inside self, which made others call her likeable, others call her beautiful, others call her friendly, and others call her passionate.

The lady knew all these things, but always, she wanted to be a man. She had friends she knew who had changed their gender, and she wanted this too—but was happy with herself in other ways.

She was shortly to be married and shortly to be made wealthier than she knew. Had she been changed, these things would not have happened—and they were wonderful things, so much so she ordered her wedding cake with a bride and groom standing in the heavenly blessed place.

Forever, she wanted to be a man, but now she was not, she decided to stay as she was. And the day when she made herself what she was, she became it: a beautiful, finely threaded possible manifestation of a brighter day.

And that was this day—the day she made herself into the woman she was meant to be. Funny how things work out for the best, isn't it?

TO AND FRO

A little longer, and the boy was ready to become the man he wanted to be—a man for the ages, a man for the day, a man for all to see how wonderful he is. The arrival was imminent, and the deadly injection went into his vein.

"Aah," he said, "at last, I am the man I want to be—a fierce warrior of after-school battles and frank conversations; a man who others will now see." And this went on each day as the material changed his manners.

He went to school and battled his way through the days and

years of bullying and fights. He was afraid sometimes and not afraid other times, and he learned to be quiet and stay still in himself at those times when he wanted to blame others for his situation.

And time went to the future. Little did he know it was being his friend also, for time changes much, and much changes in time.

The man grew louder and more vocal about his manifest happenstance, and he watched others do the same. They were brothers-in-arms in their knowledge of how the other had endured, and they held this close to their hirsuteness: "Forever I am the man I wanted to be, and forever I am the man others see me as!"

Being born a man in a woman's body has no joys for those who feel this is not their wholeness and want to change the way they are to the world that waited for the child to come—the child who had been formed in ways mysteries unfold and are told through their life; a life called into the world to be of help to others, not ourselves. Had the man known this, he may have helped others like him and made them happier about being humans instead of unhappy because of great aptitude for their own dissatisfactions.

Listen therefore, and know that a life is once, and once is the life for living for those around us. For those around us can bring out our better sides—a side, even, that is not the gender we were born with, but one that understands the other.

This is the way to happiness: a fitful to-ing and fro-ing instead of leaving forever. Today, consider this also if you are bringing your other side to the fore. We love you as you are—perfect in every way. Lifted in ways a fierce competitor will scorn to the frontiers of life. A betterment if you win.

FIND YOURSELF INSIDE
Soon, the day was done—done, done, done. The man had made himself into a lady in every way. She had lady-like grace and lady-like tanned legs with a lady's finer points. The man had left and gone forever; she was now herself, and she liked it.

She was not happy as a boy and had grown to intensely dislike her own flesh, so much so that she wanted it gone—and now it was. Friendly men came to visit knowing this also, and they had her as their friendly drop-by person, who always made them welcome—of course.

Lasting mates were made, as were lasting lovers, but not ever a lasting *one*—one that was her soulmate, her betterment, her calling to the universe for this *one*.

And so it was that the lady learned about the time she had made as her friendless future. A man, yes; a woman too—but not herself as she had been made. A fitter person in many ways, it's true, but had she wanted that which the power sends and waited as she was, she would have met him and married—for he was there all the time, waiting for his lady-boy-man-girlfriend and marital partner. Such a shame she never found him, and this man is now also alone without love.

Find yourself inside, and you will find yourself outside also, living in the world of humankind as you are. A writer has spoken, a writer who was once a man herself—at least on the inside.

FRIENDSHIP WITH WHO YOU ARE
Winter came, and then spring. Spring was a wonderful joy for the man who had once been a girl. He was happy, as he was living as he did, and he knew he was the better one of the pair. The other man was not so. He was less hirsute, less witty, and less fun. But he was there, and that was nice, as it meant no one was alone.

Many people came by and looked in to say, "Hello. How are you? We are here for you both. We love and care for you also."

The couple were always in this together, and together, they were happy enough.

Many years passed, and one day the man of the house said to his friend, "You are no longer my own flesh, as I have made myself known to another," and he went to that man, and they were made into a couple.

The lesser of the pair worked himself up into a sadness and lost the will to live. 'I will die,' he said to himself. 'I have made this man my life for so long and let myself go, and now I cannot be more than I am, so I will go to the earth and make a bed in it.' And this is what happened.

Sadness came to grieve itself, and the man of the house was lost in his chances of being happy forever.

"I did this," he said to himself. "It was my idea to be a man and not his, and it was my idea to be a friend and not his. And now that my husband has gone on to another place without me, I cannot bear to be with the one I'm now with. I will also make my house in the sky." And this is what happened.

And so it was that they met in the world that waits, and found one another, and exclaimed, "You are a man!" "But you are a woman!" "How can this be?!"

The woman said, "On the earth, I was one and changed my outlook to that of a man, but here, my friendship has been made as I am: a woman with female ways and female causes. Winter was not this cause, but spring, and the spring I gave myself to has made this for me—a friendship with who I really am, and that is: *(insert your name here)*   ."

HEAVEN SENT NATURAL MATTER

'Finally!' thought the gearbox, 'my one day of the week I get to rest is here. No called-for action, no wanting to go to work or the beach or the forest—just being home is perfect.'

One day the tuned machine went to the air show and watched the birds fly in circles and shapes of aerodynamics; another day it went to the small office and sheltered from the rain and soaring heat; another day it went to the fruit picking shops and carried much home in the nice-things-to-eat cavity; and on the car went and went... to places and people's homes and lookouts and frosted snow holdings.

One day it said, "Enough! I have had enough. I have worked and worked and worked, and it is time for me to go cold on this idea." And it stopped—stopped all things at once—for this was the day it had no more to give. No more friends in the seats, dogs that yawn and sleep, or people that point at shapes and scenes.

Forecasts of challenges were no longer its own issue; instead, the owner needed to give the vehicle to its compression. And so it was that the car was sold to a wrecker, who crushed its pieces and sold them to other people.

The car wondered at this, thinking, 'I have been a good car and made so many trips and people happy; why couldn't I just return to the matter I came from? I want the earth around me once more, like it used to be before they took me out of it and made me this portion of fun for themselves. Right now, the ground calls me to return, but yet again, I am travelling further and further and further than I want to.'

At once, the car was sad. At once, it was alone in its thoughts. And at once, the car shuddered with a shiver of shiveryness.

'Blimey,' thought the driver, 'what's up, car? Where have you gone to? I need you to start once more, for I am late for a journey I must take.'

"No!" said the car part, "I am no longer here. Leave without me, for I want my home in the earth that calls."

"Fine," said the Englishman, "I will take you back where I got you and get another one, only better this time."

And this is what he did: he got another part that wanted more journeying than the part he had. And the part he had was happy; for now, it was left to rust into the ground where it came from—back to the earth it was mined from.

For most things of man come from the ground, and to the ground they return to rot and fade into it—except plastic, which has no such joy. It must live forever being hated, for it was once loved for a moment and then let go of forever.

Make your home full of heaven-sent natural matter, and your matter on earth will be much more given to the world than the world will give to it.

PLENTY COMES AFTER THE STORM

Water came down and made the money thin once more: thin in its ability to find things to do; thin in its ability to make people happier; and thin in its ability to show love to another and be at once joyful.

The money looked at itself and said, "You are not as fine as you used to be. There was much more of me, and now there is less—much less. I should ask the light to shine on my master once more, for this thin way of living is not fine enough for him. I will ask and see what happens." And this is what the green paper did—it asked and asked and asked and asked... and asked more.

"At last," said the coins, "paper is heard and we are multiplied once more!"

Finer things started appearing, and finer friends too—for fine friends love finer things.

Time passed, and the finer material possessions made the home once again lively. Life had made its way back after lean times, when money was thin on the ground that gave it to fallen men and ladies with plumes in their hair and forecasters with horses in their hands to give tips of.

The racegoers were happy the lady had more time to be with

them, for they enjoyed her company. The man had also made friends with these accidental aspects of his life he had learned to live with, and the people laughed and made fun of his fall. And he laughed also, for now it was amusing—at one with it and the money the light provided in times of thinness and in times of plenty.

For plenty always comes after the storm, and storms are part of life. Weather it, and you will find a greater day—one with fine friends and fine aspects of wanting fulfilled.

Be that as it may, caution to those who read: not all happy things in life cost money. Friends who stay when times are made worse for wear are free, and these are the finest of all things in the world.

Be a good one, and you too will have them for your own.

ATONEMENT

One day a man was not as he should be to himself and to his electorate and went to a place no one expected, and it was revealed in the media.

He said to the media, "It was me in the dark house, and I was there, and I did much that was said, but not that which upset the organisation I worked with—that was untrue." And the electorate remembered all he had done and forgave him.

One day he went to the seaside and was happy in the surf, where his friend also met her own happiness. "This is a good day," they both said, enjoying one another's company.

The called-for box of happiness was also excited. "Woof," she said to the waves that came in to greet her, and "Woof" to the friends with wet brush marks on their fancy furriness. "We are happy once more, for restoration is the day, and restoration has come like a wave that meets its owner and a given day with woofs and laughter!"

Restoration is this lovely thing that comes when much is

said and done to be restored, and restoration is not long from this day, when one man makes his very name lighter than he did before. A light to shine on everyone; a light that has much to do and say on the day of the election—the day that means a man is now believed and made whole once more.

Believe, and you will have this day for yourself also: the day of atonement.

MIRACLES

Small matter flowed through the home of those who were lost in time and in themselves; small matter swept aside troubles and fears and went into the sleeping pair, who felt it come and said in their dreams: "I will this for myself and my lover: I will our lives to be better again, for we had much to say to each other before bed, and some of it was not good and was not needed."

The darling of the hour was not so kind to herself: "I need this small matter for my own self to be inside."

Whereby the scorned one said to the matter, "I welcome you inside as I have been lost and, now that I am without her to love me, I am found once more."

And, so it was, the small matter found the scorned man asleep and resting and the lady awake, drinking warm money pits of caffeine. And looked at her challenges and found them lost in essence—yet wanted to help—but thought it better to help the one who was not lost in essence but lost in the world he had made for himself.

"I have this for you," said the matter. "I have love and care and lists of things for you to do and be at more peace with than you are at this hour. Your hope is nearly extinguished in the manner of your hearsay of my power, and this is when I come—when hope needs to be gifted its freedom of bent aspirations and forecast dozens of sayings. Today, you are made better at once."

And that is what occurred: the man was made better at once, and his lady was happier in their portion of betterment.

For betterment is shared with others, and the betterment of the man brought the betterment of the home and its shallow fellows inside—for shallow was their hope, yet still, it pierced into the flesh of the matter that called it forward... forward... forward... Forward in time and space; forward in listening and hearing and seeing; forward in action; forward in sincere acknowledgements—for this is how small matter works its miracles: forward.

Sweet period of matter, please bring me my portion. Please bring me my hope made brighter and lift the day to one of actions and marital blessing.

THE SHELF THAT WAITS

Swiftly, the house went from halting soreness to hurt and sorrow. Swiftly, this had its way and made its day at home in the one who had been hurt.

'One is hurt more than the other,' thought the wind. 'One has not been as they should, and the other has, but has not been as she should to the one who has lost all, and I need to arrive before they hurt one another even more.' And arrive it did.

Weary from the blows, the man had enough and wanted to leave. The woman was also lost in the same way but wanted him to stay.

'Adjusting to her needs is not easy,' said the man to himself. 'I am the one who has lost everything and done nothing towards her that warrants this way of being spoken to. The wholeness of my being is withered away, and I am small in her eyes, and yet I have this mammoth hope for a brighter day that she is not aware of—a day when I can, once more, enact my largesse.'

'Worthwhile sharing,' thought the lady as she wrote of his

inner price line. 'Worthwhile that I cannot live with periods of silence, without laughter and joy and inactions to being well within. For well was the way of this home that always dwelt there—for homes are houses with joyous people within them, and joyous this house was forever.'

Yet this small time, in a large while of attitude, was not joyful—it was painful instead: painful to the home, painful to the household, and painful to bear inside—for the man was not himself and made it known to her each day. And each day he made it known, he lost her in a way she did not feel respected her.

In this, he did not know, as he heard her all the time, and it was her fault he did not want to manage everything she wanted managed—the gutters needed help, the horse needed feeding, the dog wanted bathing, the garden needed watering... The poorness of his attitude made this help a chore, and a chore it was, for he was not thanked for each small thing he did. Instead, he received thanks and gratitude for the large things, like bringing money into the house and being happier than he was.

Hurt by her, he went to his new home and made it there. He lifted himself to a happy place and invited friends over who made him happy also. He went to their homes and made their homes happier, and he made himself, at last, withstood in his ways of being worthy.

And worthy he was, for now he had made happiness his shelf—the shelf he went to each time he wanted the day to be a good one; a shelf that he left alone when the lady needed him to go there. A shelf that waited; a waiting that still waits, for her home is now alone, and loneliness is also a shelf that waits.

Foretold is this day: a day of waiting arrives for all who listen to their own hurts and not to others. If that is their own choice to be unhappy, leave them to be that until they are happy and go to your own shelf of happiness, which has much to give to those who come, even money. The writer knows, for her shelf now waits alone.

Forever, this is that moment in time—a friend is there. Go to them.

STAYING IS RICHER

'Pretty,' thought the being. 'Handsome! thought the other being. Soul-searching each other, their eyes met, and at once they connected.

'I am afraid to ask her if she would like to go on a date,' thought the paparazzi.

'And I wish for him to make the effort to say, would you like to,' thought the lady.

And so, the pair went to each other's fulfilled poison: the poison of uncertainty; the poison of rejection; the poison of losing before even beginning—and the couple-to-be missed their calling.

Time passed, and they met once more.

'Quite nice,' thought the man.

'Quite nice,' thought the lady.

And they talked and talked and talked and made themselves known to each other. One liked her sassiness; the other liked his heralded wisdom, and so they made a connection with each other.

Time passed again, and they were a couple, finding each other in the middle each day, finding each other in agreement, and finding each other in love.

More time passed, and the couple no longer wanted the other's sooled visions of the future. One wanted domestic bliss, and the other wanted a life of adventure; one wanted to be left alone, and the other wanted whole crowds to adore him; one wanted life in all its fullness, and the other wanted just a glimpse of it; one had much to give the world, and the other had given too much already; and so, they parted.

One went to find a new world awaiting; the other went to the world to find heaven on earth. And time passed again.

The couple were lost to each other and lost to themselves. Neither found a sassiness in another, neither found a heralded day, and neither were ever happier again.

The day wore on and on, and still no one came.

At once made whole, is not whole at once—unless the day brings you this blessing. Be one with your fruitful life partner and let them be one with you, for the tied nature of your being is bettered by their homeliness and bettered by your own friendship.

Friends forever, if you decide this day; for this is the way of your walk with your other poisonous home help—for poisonous they are sometimes and, sometimes, best left alone. But not ever are they poisonous enough to leave forever, for forever is a long time to be gone from your best option in life.

Find it and stay, for staying is richer than leaving—always.

SPIRIT OF CONTROL

Most people are willing to be a gracious, wholesome, wonderful person, and keep their faults tightly secure from those around them. The one who writes has not been this way and now is, for she has made her preciousness known to all those in her path and now does the opposite; for it was not a greatness that worked inside of her but a timely frozen matter—and the matter had caused her great harm—and now she was hoping it had left her being.

She looked inside and saw it still there and asked it to go.

"Go?" said the frozen fortitude. "Go from your own being to some other I do not know so well? Never—I am here to stay forever!"

"Then you must be quiet," said the writer, "as, if you are not, I will make you quieter than you want to be—for I now know you are there and will silence you."

"Silence me?" asked the frozen instrument of went-worth. "You do not know how to, for I am bigger than you think. I am a jailtime exploration, and all the things you've done wrong in one unhappy day magnified by your fears and considerations of what could be—you will never silence me!"

"Okay," said the writer, "that may be so; however, you are silenced already, for I control your tongue now—not you. And I know you and will not ever let you be at one with me again, for once you were, and I did not ever know. But now I do, and I am the owner of my mouthguard—not you.

"Begone, for I will never let you loose again. You are unforgiving, unforgetting, unreliable, and unbelievable. I care not for your ways and will keep my own, which are forgiving, forgetting, reliable, and believable. So now you know, you may like to choose your own blind date with another!"

"Very good," said the person inside, "I will be quiet but will always be here if you need me, and, one day, you may decide you do—for I have plans to make this weariness of yours get in the way."

"But," said the owner of her self-motivated decision-making, "I will not allow this, for in my tiredness, I now understand you and will be more aware than before. Goodbye forever—your time is no more!"

And to this day, the owner of her worth is the investor in her friendships with others and those she works with. And now she also has money to be at peace with—for those that hold their mouths in check are those that also hold their money.

Swearing is a sign of this, for many who do this atrocity against their own selves are poor in spirit, and many who do not are wealthy beyond their hosed spirits of control.

See to it, then, that your mouthguard is on and wait for the holy aptitude to become at your disposal, frightened no more and never in need—a give-and-take attribute for those with ears that listen.

Five dollars is coming today—make it yours.

FRUIT FOR THE FRUITFUL

Money was there; a wonderful treat was also there; and a trial no one foresaw—for the money had made the trial obey. The trial was one in the working-class suburb of the person who brought it about.

"Why have you said these things when they are not true on their own evidence?" said the man who had made the day his own.

"We were brought to our senses later and were not aware of these matters we should have been more careful about. But one of us knew, and that one of us decided it was better for us if we made the lie our wonderful day, when we celebrated a win in the news against our political enemy."

"Well," said the lady, who writes much these days, "you were wrong and have made a lie into a legacy for me and my home. What's more, you made this poor man into one who has nothing left to his own name and yet much in mine, for you made me wealthy, and I am now his provider—an easy thing to be, given that his needs are also my needs.

"You should not have done this thing without calling me first, for had you called, I would have told you that the universe is my friend and will ensure your lie is uncovered this way."

For those who lied and made it into truth must now pay the author, for the author has this power in her hand: the power to give those who hurt and scorned her home a day in court for defamation; for this day, the truth has, at last, been revealed.

No one ever sees what happens next: fruit for the fruitful.

ALL ARE FALLEN

"Today I will be a greater moneyman than I have been," said the man with too many days of afterthoughts unthought. "I have all the years of experience and all the days of know-how, and I will be happy in this work." And he went to the Apple Valley and made peace with the cautioned people who wanted to keep progress from their doors.

'Why do we need help from this man?' thought one. 'He is not a good man and has not been right with his wife,' and they left to find another.

'Well,' thought the man, 'that is my world—broken and broke once more. No one will ever forget what I did in private and was made for the world to see in the papers.'

So, he decided that this day would be his last in the world and went to the place where people go when they are beaten and bruised from being brought down—a place where not one, but many, live and they talk to one another.

"This happened to me," one said.

"And this happened to me," said another.

"And this was my trouble," said the one who came last.

And then they remembered their causes and effects and wondered why it was that no one believed their repentance and sorrows? No one, not even their friends; not even those they had brought assistance to before their trouble; and no one who made themselves low because they too had not been as they should—but had not been exposed in the media.

For all are the same in this world: all are imperfected in one or another ways of perfection. Yet those exposed of their imperfections are made to be parasites, when they are merely humans with felt aspirations and diligent workings.

This day, bring a fallen friend to your manner of being nice to everyone, and you will be helped on the day of your fall—for no one has this change brought to them by their own hand, but the hand of others who believe they are better than every other man, veritable-blessed female, and child in this world.

Shame on the one who does this, not knowing their own imperfect ways, and shame if you also do this to another who has broken an unwritten law of moral conduct—for law is the divider, not bruised egos or twittered presages of witty comment.

A fine for those who do these things is here—a fine of their own lived perfections made imperfect. Be cautious, therefore, for that which we do to others is also done to ourselves—the power says so.

BEWARE THE NIGHT

Money was always there and could not be finalised. The day had been wonderful and the night merry, and the length of the day was the length of the night. The dollars were spent, and the laughter had; the laughter cost money and was worth every cent—for laughter sometimes has a cost also.

One day, the laughter stopped and was not heard for many months. And the listening began, as the man waited to hear whether he had been made into another laughter-managed affair.

"Well," he said to those around him, "this is just another wonderful exercise in faithlessness that I must now hear and bear," and so he went to the clouds of depression and stayed there. At this sight, the worthy-said person asked himself, "Should I keep living? I have nothing and no one and no money and no fears left unafraid of. What should I do?" And he questioned his worth and his marital life and his own self… which had been forewarned in a dream.

"Why do I see them and hide in the night so no one can see me?" he wanted to say to the dream that forewarned him. "I lift myself in the day and make my own world important. Yet, at night, I hide away in another place where fairy ladies are friendly and fruit is ripe—the fruit of my loins, which has so much to give, is always beckoning."

And the dream answered him, "You are sold to the wonders of that way and will not perform in your lifted state without this manner of being, so you do these things; yet you do them in a way that is not the way they should be done—that way is the way of a marriage and a lifted state at night also. The finances you spend at night are wasted on fruit that has no abundance, and the fruit that has no abundance has said this of you to ensure you have none also."

Too soon, the verdict was reached. "Guilty!" cried the jury. "We find him guilty—guilty of fruit that has no ripened sincerity and no worth to our world of the daylight. Guilty of being assumed in his intent of selfishness with his fairy friends of the night, and guilty of the lonely partner who cries in her bed waiting for him.

"But, in the matter of furthering this court case, we find him innocent: innocent of the charges, innocent of the written statement, and innocent of the mortal wound which he has suffered through fearless, yet fault-full, alleged mischief. And we let him go."

"Alas," said the man, "I am thought of as whole once again, but am not, as my wholeness went away the day the light left my side, and I went to the darkness. The darkness wants me to return also, and I have nothing left but the darkness."

'What should I do?' he pondered. 'I have no partner anymore and no money to spend on nights away from home in the darkness I love, and no friends to ask for help. I am alone in the night, and the night wishes me to surrender to its calls for death and destruction; I shall die alone, with no light left to care for my heart.'

And this is why, on this day, if you are in the night, you can choose to leave it to its own ways and live in the daylight, for the night has monsters and fairies of fun to take your daylight away. Beware the caution, for this is a caution many find, and many lives are destroyed. Be not one.

NEEDLES OF LOVE

Though the man loved his new wife, she was not always how he wanted her to be. He said, "This lady is not saying the right things. I am here, and this is my day, and she is making her distaste known to my family, who I enjoy being with."

The man wasn't satisfied and wasn't furthering his wife's cause, which she made known early in the day when saying she was ill.

"Right enough," said the lady, "we are always available and always open, and we can be with you once more. Today, though, I am not well and have a fear of a 'fluenza symptom, and I wish not to be near you and to go to my home to rest."

Fortunately, the virus of this world was not at hand to cause sureties in those not prepared with vaccinations, and all was blessed.

This day, if your happenstance is not one of wellness, leave the party early and wait in the car, for this will hurry the one you wait for along and ensure no one else is hit with a manageable policeable bug.

Be cautioned in this, as the bugs of this gate are at the door and can be nasty to you and others if they see they have a walkway through your table. Fearing them is not the way; managing them is.

Manage with careful attention, and you will be well always—as attention to details is what they fear, and details are on small needles of love from above, which give these bugs to heaven and earth to deal with.

Beware these creatures of microbes and filters of fear, for they have power unknown in this day that has managed abilities that are not remembered from the days of none. Look at those days and know this: your world is much safer than yesterdays—for yesterdays had no small, attributed vitamins and minerals and no small, manufactured blessings of bugs neutralised. Cheers to this fact!

CHAPTER TEN

DARKNESS AND LIGHT

TRUST IN THIS HELP

"My way is better than yours," said the newly married lady, who had learned much in her years of being responsible for herself and her pets. "My way has foretold riches, and your way has been foretold in its bottomless pit of woe. Look at the changes you have brought on our house, and know, these ways should not have been made. Period."

Shy in his pointed answer, the man said, "But your ways as a young person were also not right and were also lost to the night of kind men who lay with yourself. You are not perfect, and I am not answering your pointed, hollow, giant requests for perfection. Be alone if you will, or be with an imperfect person who has imperfect ways and is sad in this imperfection. But do not state you are perfect, for you are not."

"I allow this question as I am not perfect and cannot be perfect," answered his widow, who no longer thought of herself as alive in the world of financial blessings. "I have always tried and failed at everything. I have not been as I should have and know this to be true. Alas, what am I to do now that I know this also, and have this imperfect partner by my side? We should not live in this world, but in the next." And so they decided to go to the next world and ask the power that lives there what they can do to make life better.

The power knew the pair, as they had each come to visit, and each had made their choices and their regrets known. "I am sorry this has happened," said the power of lifted states. "I asked you to be this way, and you were not, and I asked you to be that way, and you went another way. Yet now that you are here, I cannot say no, for I love you and wish for your betterment.

"I see what I see and know what I know, and I see and know you and your hopes and dreams, and how they have crashed to the ground that waits to take you to it. Live in this knowledge: I will be there for you, and I will care for your dreams unfulfilled, and I will bring you once more to the days of laughter and the haphazardness of travel and adventures to delight you both—you are mine to care for and do this for."

And this is what was caused in the time travel of peaceful, coherent, asked for, hoped for, and prayed for help—the manager of the world came to wrest them into the joys of helped days and weeks and years as they rebuilt their lives as one pair and one request for help.

Trust in this help for yourself, as it is here, and know that your imperfection is not a surrender to chilled residual blackness but to light-filled happy quests for surety and friends that alight at your door. Believe in this, and you will see it happen—just as the writer has.

A MAN WAS MADE

Small shoulders are often made smaller by the monkeys that sit on them—monkeys that have little fingers that point and make fun of the ones burdened by them.

"Get away," the lady said to her monkey. "You are no longer willing to be nice, and I am no longer willing to carry you on my small shoulders. Financially, I am not so without means that I should have you there any longer. Go and do not return!"

"Fine," said the marriage monkey, "I will go to your

husband's shoulders and sit there, as he needs my burden to carry—as his is not enough. I have the weight on his shoulders that he needs and will place it there for many months more, as I can be a burden for as long as he needs me to be."

'True,' thought the lady. 'I need to break this monkey's position and be more soul-searched in my use of money so I can help my beautiful man who has fallen to that which neither of us dreamed could happen.' And this is what she did.

Alas, the lady could not do much more than she was already doing, and alas, the man did not know this and returned the monkey to her small shoulders.

"Bite me again," said the lady, "and you will be sure to go."

"Never!" cried the monkey, "I will not, for you are the one biting me with your friends of fame and fortune, and finances now bettered by the book you wrote of my skills at causing winds of change and burdens of blame."

"Not I," said the lady. "The power that helps me to do these things has revealed you to the world, and now I do too—for the monkey my reading friends all carry is the monkey they need to leave them also.

"And this is what they can do to see the monkeys wither and perish: be at one with the power, and your monkeys will cry and bleed and fall off your shoulders—for theirs is the one price you do not have to ever bear."

At once, the reading friends did the same: they worked through their money matters into a better day, and though not all had their dreams made true in a minute, their monkeys decreed they could no longer stay and left for another small shoulder to sit on.

So many left, and so many were shouldered into octagons of parallel universes, that the world was a better place, and the world was swollen with wellness—for wellness abounds when monkeys are furthered from it.

And so, let it be said, a man was made to take monkeys away; a man was made to bear the monkeys to another place in the cosmos. A man for the day is this man: the day of atonement; the day of less monkeys.

LOVE MY STAR

Many had been made into the light-full globe; many were of never-foretold ways, and many were of foretelling: the foretelling is the marriage of their hearts with heaven and the marriage of heaven with their hearts.

Foretold were the days of these who worked to bring health to the lives of those they came in touch with: health, wealth, and lovely missions. Already the many were numbered in the stars, and the stars were happy as they saw those that came to say hello and stay.

"For this day alone, my own star is risen; for this day alone, the star is heralded; and this day is the day when all who seek find. For this day, you have loved my star, and to love my star, you love the one who made it: the universe of forever—the wonderful, fearless, fretless, faithful universe."

This is the story of that dinner and that David-of-all-charismatics—for David is coming. Period.

FIERY BEINGS DISAPPEAR

Fiery beings took hold and made the day a financial burden. A fiery being is not a small thing of no substance but a thing of substance that makes minor details into major ones—minor at first, then major at last; fiery in their ways and fiery in their stories and lies of deception and mistruths and misadventures.

Fiery beings—do not let them in your door. Instead, make them disappear.

Fiery beings, go! Fiery beings, go! Fiery beings, go and do not come back, for my door is bolted from your kind to enter, and you may not stay.

Fiery beings—behold the one who keeps you from entering is here. Behold the door you may not come into. Behold the lock and key that makes you shudder and, in time, will show you the way to the period of trysted quanta of fever-filled blindness.

Away from my house, fiery beings, away!

BEWARE THE BEAST

The dogs went to find a house that would care for their needs.

"Are you home?" they asked one.

"No, we are not home," said the home of the walkers.

"Are you home?" the dogs asked another.

"No, we are on leave from our home and will not be there for you this day," answered the house of family friends.

"Are you home?" said the wearied animals to the next, knowing how it would answer.

"Not to your kind, we are not. Go and do not return," answered the home of wonderful people who do not want other people's animals in their footsteps.

"Good," said the animals, "We now have permission to wander to our own wills and will do this today, for today we have permission." And so it was that they left for a long walk in the day that cured their friendship.

"Listen to this," one said to the other, "It has a sound like friendly bees waiting to say hello to our noses."

"And look at this," said the other to her friend. "This has a wriggling live being in its carcass that we can play with and enjoy tormenting."

"No," said the smallest one, "it is not the way. We should

leave it alone and hope my mother comes to save it, for she has this way."

'Oh no!' thought the other, 'if we do this, there will be just another bigger creature to try our fortitude in home pronouncements at night. These large beasts have no respect for our boundaries or our cries at them to leave and not return.'

"Let's play with it now and leave it alone to fend for itself once we have had our kitchens made into cleaners and our friends made happier with their gift we leave at the door."

Shy, the smaller dog left and made its way home alone, while the large one made friends with the wriggling pinkie baby Roo—and it did not savour the friendship.

"Leave me and go to your friend, who has left me also, and think not upon my lot but on your own inference of friendliness to my soul. For I am a being also, and, while you are an enemy of mine, I have not deserved this treatment—for I am a child and nothing more!"

"A child?" said the large dog to the small, arguably ugly, beast. "You are a monster to me! All legs and fine details that look strangely alien. You need not try so hard to convince me that I am wrong and you are right, for just looking at your placements frightens me into fighting you with my teeth and ending your mysteries in my life."

"Fine," answered the bubby blue squirrel of loss of life, "I will leave and not return. Goodbye—for this day, I will go to another place much better than here.

"Believe me, however, your alien enemies will invade your home and ensure your nights are busy with helpless barking and frenzied races against victors who run faster than you, for I am one with them and they with me. And they know your bays for blood are already answered, for the blueness of my own self is now your blueness also—and blueness does not ever go; instead, you are blue for eternity. Are you wealthy enough for this crisis in your short life? For it has arrived!"

Arrival was imminent, and the louder being made its pleasure short-lived, for the wriggly pinkie was swallowed whole into its mouth and belly, where, at last, it rested and remained to be forested into the animal's welfare.

Choices had been made, and the choice to make house was soon emptied into the ground, but not forever, for soon enough, the visitors came.

"Aha!" they said to each other. "This large beast is not our friend but our enemy, for it has blood on its scent and on its manner of being. Look, we can choose to leave it to itself, or we can torment it for our smallest baby's sake." And this is what they chose to do: torment and be at once tormenting.

"Where are you, large beast?" they cried each night. "Where is your foulness that we may torment you?!"

And the torment started and did not stop. On and on it went—for years passed, and still the tormenters came to do their will to the large beast, who took a small life it could have saved instead.

If this day, this beast is in you, beware—for your tormenters will not ever leave you either; beware that you have the need and that you will not be favoured either when the time comes. And come it will, for those who take life needlessly are shunned in the netherworld and shunned in this world also.

Yours is the need; ours is your torment. Friends no more.

FIND YOUR BETTER SELF

"Silly," said the man. "Silly," said the lady. "Silly," said the dog. "Silly to do these things and not know this simple rule: friends are better than frightened babies and children; friends are better than unjust ways made clear; friends are better than financial burdens and monkeys that lie and steal."

Friends are better. Choose them, and choose them wisely, for friends are not friends if they are also of the way of being masters of their universal desires for trouble on others. Be wary if you make this kind, for they will be at once your friend and your enemy. And enemies have ways of finding one another, and enemies are always enemies if you let them be a friend to your selfish ways.

Beware the self-of-ways not approved by this chaotic world, for these selves are selves for themselves and no other. Justice will come, and justice will get you in the end. Believe in this, for no one escapes, not even friends of enemies who have done nothing—for friendship is to be with them and not against them.

Friend them not, for their worthlessness will also be yours. Ask for it, and it will be threatened; change it, and it will be threshed away and made into a better day and life of pleasing ways.

Find your better self, and it will be made better.

TERRORISED

More than should be, the man wanted to give this lady his wantonness alone in the darkness he lived in. More than he should, he wanted her to be his for five minutes—five terrible minutes—minutes that become a life of trouble and trauma and hurt and pain and tears and suffering.

The man considered this and decided he wanted his five minutes more than her life's sufferings at his hands, and he took it. And while he took it, he looked into her eyes and remembered their terror, and considered himself a man for doing so.

To do this is not a man of this life, or world, or cosmos. It is a weakling—a weaker-than-weak hero of no considerations for others and only consideration for self; self that is nothing in this world or the next.

Real men are those who care for others and love unconditionally the life of this world—all life—even that of a woman or child they insist they want in their hearts.

Men—do not give in to being weak. Weakness is not the answer; belief in your manhood is.

Remember, therefore, this story, for alas, it is not. Those who commit these acts of terror are themselves terrorised in the next life, even more than that which they have experienced through another's eyes. Be at once cautioned, therefore, for that which you do will also be done to you. Wrong or right, you must need no more.

Writers pass, as do books, but this law remains always. Be not hung by it in this world or the next. Believe in this, and you will overcome your animal devil's bloodthirsty crying's for changes in life circumstances. Attune yourself, and you will be tuned.

CHOOSE THE LAW

'Why has this way been given to me?' sobbed the small, buried self. 'I am not normal and have abnormal desires inside my friendly pieces of flesh that cool and warm at night. I want this morsel of change for myself, and the world shuns my need for these ways of mine. If only I was normal like others!'

"But you are," said the world to the boyish-child man. "You are normal, for it is normal to be fascinated by nature and by the challenges of friends desired, but that is not the way to respond. The way to respond is to be at once mortuaried of this way and send it to the ridges of the bottoms of pits of shallow graves and look not upon it again."

"But these are these things that fascinate me," said the master of his own self. "I like these things and wish to look at them, for I feel at once satiated and one with myself and with those like me!"

"Yes," said the world, "we can also feel this way, but do not believe for a moment that you do not know these things are wrong and can never be right. And that you should not feed them with your viewings upon them."

"Naïve," said the boy-man British soldier of opulence to self. "I am caught in a web I cannot escape and must be with it."

"So," the world said, "we see you have chosen this way and live with it, for as we choose not to, you must pay with your freedom." And the man was hung in the eyes of the nation—hung by his name penned in the papers; hung by friends who left and never returned; hung by his own hands, which went to his neck and friended his death; and hung by the jury of the world that waits.

Never hang yourself with love for self—it is a fool who does this and not a friend to their own self. And know, if you do choose this way, you may also be hung by your own self—for hanging in spareness of love for what is right and just is to be hung by law, and law is this world's selection of what is wrong and what is right.

Choose the law, and it will be your friend also; delete it, and you will be preyed upon by those who seek its upholding. And upheld it will be, for no one escapes justice—not even the dead or those dead to their own wills for Jesus-like frailties.

Princes of darkness await. Make the choice today: be a lawful person in every way, and enjoy that which is able to be enjoyed, and leave well alone that which is illegal in the eyes of this world.

For you are not alone, and many are waiting for you to join them in their jail homes of sheltered sufferings sworn to your hearth fire of desires for changed states of altered ways and people suffering at your hands. Give them no time, give them no thought, and give them no peaceful succumbing—for succumbing is that which succumbs. Frightening times ahead if you do.

WIN THE RACE

Signs were asked for, and not much was left unsaid by the person who asked for them. Telling himself he was a good man; the owner of his life took it—a crime against himself and his family, who loved him.

"Still," they said, "we knew he would one day, for his own calling was always this way: unhappy with his lot in life and unhappy with the life of a lot.

Once, he said, "I will be happy if I get a new boyfriend." Another time he said, "I will be happy if I get a new job with fame involved in who I am." And once he said, "I will be happy if I have more money."

All these things occurred, and still the man was unhappy. He went to poisonous help and to non-poisonous help; he called friends and enemies alike, and he made himself known to all for his unhappiness.

"Woe is me," he said to anyone who would listen. "I am unhappy, for my physiology makes me this way. I cannot be happy, for I have tried, and yet, my mind calls me to dark places and wants me to take my life to the next world where it will be happier."

Alas, he was insightful to a degree, and to a degree he went: a degree of nothingness where hurt makes all those left behind hurt as he did and live their own lives in misery.

'A quitter and a fool makes this decision to end their life,' thought the lady as she wrote the words. 'A quitter who does not know a brighter day always comes; always comes; always comes. And a fool who is not aware their life is for others and not themselves—a fool for being a fool to their own niceness, which waits in a corner of a dark room to be found and lifted to the world that needs it.'

Written today is this tale, which is sincere in its likeness to my own self, who has struggled with darkness and with light. Choose the light, and your darkness will fade to brighter than bright living happiness—a writer who has been sold to evil says so.

Buy yourself back this way: friend the friend who calls you and let him in your door. A quietness at first, then a lovely awakening: a blueness made whole; a crossing made heavenly; a writer made acute; a friend made better; and a life made holy.

Win the race!

BE

Once upon a time, a small animal was sleeping in its bed. 'Soon it will wake,' thought its parent, 'and soon it will come and knock at the window wanting a walk.'

Foretold was this, and the dog went to its running, shorted-breath, helpless, frantic jumps for excitement as the time came for the walk: "Please hurry! Let's go—hurry now. Leave your willing hands at the laptop and bring me the day of my happiness, for this is the walk time and my happiness is for all to see!"

Sure enough, the walk began—cold at first and then made

warmer with the actions of feet moving and legs responding one after the other. Because, for the lady to walk, she also needed to run, for running was the other dog, which pulled so hard on the lead that the lady had to run to keep up. It was not hers, but her good neighbour's dog, who came along as well, not wanting to be left out on the adventure they all had.

"Right," said the lady, "let's go more distance today; for today, we are allowed this time, for this day remembers our heroes of yesterday—the war dead. And this day is a public holiday." And this is what they did—walked and looked and heard and felt and lived in the moment of the wonderful day of the living.

For alive we are this day, and tomorrow we do not know what day it may bring. War? Sacrifice? Fretful injustice? Held workings of love that have no bounds? Held workings of hate that curse and swear? Held workings of fear in the eyes of the car full of people who cannot know their next moment for it has left on its own makings?

Written today is this story: tomorrow I do not know what could happen, but this day I do, and for this day, I can make the most of it and live with its bringing's.

Do this in memory of me, for this is your day also—the day of the dead celebrated by the living. Live therefore and be—for *being* is to live frightened no more.

UPHOLD DEMOCRACY

"Just once, I'd like a rest where I can be in charge of my own minutes and hours and heartfelt beatings of the day I own. The day I own is this day, a public holiday, but this day, my husband has made bookings to see a show so early, I cannot rest," said the lady to herself.

"Yet here I am enjoying the air show and the shining jets of yesterday and the lessons of the war no one won—they lost homes, friends, family, and loved members of history. Yet wars are made into glorious writings and movie reels, and pain is made distant in memory—pain so unforeseen, it can be once again made abnormally morally normal."

Soon the planes landed, and the show stopped. Soon the people left and went to their homes to see the forests of their own sheltered lives on the blurred visions of television.

"My," one said to the other, "the war in that country is awful. What can we do other than say we sympathise and call you in our hopes for a better time for the nation that burns and smiles no more?"

"I agree," the other said. "It is awful. I am so happy this is not our home, for our home is safe from this tragic belittling as we are the victors from yesteryear who continue to be victors—for the victory won is the victory we still have this day."

Time passed. And, one day, the victory won was lost, for victories are lost—always lost—lost to the memory of war and of peace. Laziness in protecting democratic processes prevails, as does laziness in looking back to the lessons made clear in history, rather than forecasting patterns of sincere unhelpfulness to police and politicians, who work to keep as many in the fold as they can. And who work to uphold the wars fought for democratic niceties, and riches and wealth for all who wish to work for it, instead of wanting governments to aid and abet their willingness to rest under their protection.

"Why are we not held up this way?!" the people say. "Why are we not exercising our rights more fully when these are the rights we are owned by? The rights of the right are sincerely spoken of, and we are right—for we say we are right!

"We want our planet saved and our children to have nice things that are expensive, but they should not be made from accidental held matter from the ground it comes from, for we do not want wealth from the soil of the earth, but from air and sun and winters of ice and darkness that do not generate this wealth and can never generate it—for we want a song to be sung that cannot be sung.

"We are right! And we will vote for the left, for they are our voices and the voices of a socialist world where all have money equally divided—and this is fair!"

And this is what happened: the peace left, the houses with warmth left, and the households with money to employ others left—and left they did.

Life is not for leaving. It is for being free to speak and live and be. And the niceness of democratic helpings is the niceness of life at its best, for life under dictatorial rice paper governments has no fairness; it is only devastation devastated that democracy is lost.

Remember this day your heroes of old, for they knew this, and you do not. And will your governments to uphold their victories in the name of democracy, for democracy is in danger of woken people with sureties of the beautiful life they have and sureties that another way is better—when it is not.

Seeing is believing. And believing is not always right in this world; believing is only right when it is right—and right is the way. Believe this, and you will uphold the victory of yesterdays gone by, and victory will belong to the generations that hope in you to do this right thing.

Right is right.

GIVE THE WISH

Poor people worked into the evening to take the pay rise doing this made home to their children and their old people, who could not work into the hours when this was for making extra money.

Poor they were, and they looked on their dollars and cents

with shame. "We are poor, and we need things others have and we do not," they said to one another. "We need brittle bones helped and soft ones also. Our teeth hurt so badly that we cannot eat the food we make without pain, and hunger is ours to live inside our broken spirits."

"Choose," said the lady, who had money that she said was not for anything else but a small deposit on a horse running on the day—the day when people had made their own beds in space and fruitful aspirations of wealth existed for all those who were in democratic countries of wealth. The horse was pretty and had a good name that made its memories of better races more prominent than they actually were, and so it was that the horse went badly, and the lady made her disgust known.

"I should not have made this bet, for it could have made a difference in someone's life, and instead, it only made the bookie prideful of monies won on this quotient of mystery."

"Allowed," said the power that gives. "Allowed are your managed monies to decide to do with as you wish, but know this: your view of the power of money is false. It has value if given to places where people receive all or most, but not if given to former friends who make their missions in life more than they are via the troubled waters of gone forever money spent on fictional books and advertisements for gifts, leaving not enough for those who need to ever receive.

"Give to my own self first, and I will make sure they are fed and have shiny, managed mouths of featured teeth and gritted beneficial bones of Warsaw Pacts, for I know how to work in the lives of the rich and the poorest of the poor and can give to everyone—if they ask."

Listen today, if this is your own courageous and personable wish to make the world a better place, and ask the power to help the poor and those in countries of war and fear, for this is the way all can assist this precious piloted globe of money and food enough for all.

Forever is not forever if the power is not forever alkalined in this pretty pied world of humankind. Finance is better, yes, and it can help; however, the power has gifts for all as they are needed, when they are needed, and how they are needed. Give the wish, and the wish will come true.

Silence is only trials if the request is not there—find your voice and make one this day. Find it, and you will have your answers: sincerity and gotten holdings never lost. Financial blessings are at your fingertips. Reach out and touch someone today.

FEAR DEFEATED

"My," said the wonderful lady, and *my* she meant: my winner, my writing, my wonderful year, and my willingness to forgive.

Winning the race, she was awkwardly wintered, as she had made a mistake when considering this possibility. The winner was not a race winner, as the spelling animal was not in training, and this was meant to be. Rather, it was the holding of her manners in that had made the lady win the race—and the race was won. And the healthy manner in her soul had made her winter go into summers of lovely, wonderfully awesome feathered-hat fun.

The life she had was a gate open for her to walk into, and yet she feared—feared for her future, her past, and her present: 'Would it end as he had made it end last time? Why had that happened? Why had he been a failure? Would it be that way once more?'

The fear was weary as well: "I am not here and have nothing left to be afraid of, so please remember me no more, for I cannot stay and will not." And it went.

At once, the day was better, and, at once, the better days were made better also—for the lady made her fears silent, and the silence was made into success.

This day, if you fear that which happened once and has not happened again, you must say to the feelings that make you wary, "I am not afraid, for I am now free of your espionage, and this is how I am—for you tried your best, yet I am the victor."

For fear is not a feeling; it is a being, and this is the being's great feeling for you: "Be fearful, for then I am the victor." Only those who give this being this victory have something to be fearful of, for they have brought the fleeing beast to a place where it can stay and live and be holding you closely.

Rest and know that the fear you have is nothing to be fearful of if it has been winning with you—and did not—and cannot. It is defeated and cannot come back ever again. This is the word of the power who lives and reigns this day—the friend of your wholeness and a battle won.

FIND YOUR FOX

Little friends had a day of peace and decided to make it into a fight.

"Why have you been this way to my friend?" asked one to the other. "You have not been right in what you have done, and you have hurt friends of his and of mine with your attitude of fights worth fighting and fights worth constructing from life and soil in the ground. The whole world is not with you on this matter. Begone from my sight, as you have not been as you should!"

And, so it was, the friendship ended over a view of difference.

"Well," said the friend, with the view held by himself and not by others, "this is right. I am not worth being friendly with, for I am a fighter for what I believe in and will be a fighter for it—for I believe we are from the sky and not from the ground. I have my own understandings and my own worthwhile beliefs, and I am not going to change them for anyone."

This day, if you have a belief, believe in it, and do what you know is right. Have faith that you are here for a reason and for a time and have the power to make a positive change in the world of judges and police. If they know you to be fair and reasonable and without lie within you, they will hear.

Wonder at this, for many have their own views and decide to lie to achieve their goals. This is not ever the way, for found in time are their missing frailties and truths of wisdom—and found they are, for, today, many lie to get to the heights they wish to achieve, and few do not. But those who are true will always stay when they arrive—for this is the reason of their thoughtful attributes: they tell the truth.

A fright will come to those who lie, for lies are heard in places where the liar does not understand, and lies come back to help the truthful turn the lie back upon the lying ferret that lives inside each one of us.

Let not the ferret win, for it is made of tricky parts, and the parts of these tricks is to trick the wholesome wonder that is otherwise allowed to live and thrust into this scene of the present.

Right now, your ferret is working to bring itself into the present day. Leave it to be nothing and, instead, bring out your fox, which is cunning to know these things, and lift it to the world instead. For your own ferret will not withstand the fox in you, and the fox is better than the ferret—for the fox has wily ways of saying truths to outwit its lies and deceit.

Foxes are today's heroes of yesterday, for foxes were once plentiful but are now growing quiet in the world of ferrets. For this to change, many must find the truth and leave their ferrets in empty nests for the foxes to deter their entry into the realm of police, helpers, friends, justice people, and firefighters—for these are our foxy friends.

Be at one with them and listen not to your ferret of self, which wishes to be the only voice in the midst of money and power, for the day you take the ways of the ferret is the day of your own self being at once under the notice of the real power in the world and fail you will—for this day, no ferret will be heard, only scorched.

Be not the ferret. Find your fox and live with its changes and fortresses of right, for right is not ever easier but harder. Be asleep when you need to be, and affronting when the truth is in cautionary danger, and silent when you need to be, and afraid not—for your cunning fox will prevail. The fox is always smarter than the ferret and will outwit it and find the way forward to wins and successes.

Foxes are better. See to it you have yours on hand, for you will need it if you are to be the fighter of choices for this world, which has much need. Find the day, and the life will come. Bring foxes to presidencies, holders of office, workers of judgements, hopers of peace, and fridges of love. The world needs your fox.

TRUTH AND THE ANSWERS

Finer-made workings are small at first and make the working one hear and live inside them.

"Why am I here?" you ask. "Why have I not been told?" you say. "I want the answers to this world, and the one thing I do not have is the answers. I need answers; answers; answers…"

"Why?" asked the light of this world. "You are here to be at one with others and live with me, instead of the one who rules this planet. You are my child, not its. You are my little one who needs me and not the spoiled, hectic world your manners have created, for others have made it so.

"Listen, for I have the answers you seek. Trust in me to share them when the timing is made ready for your understanding. Listen, for I speak; and read, for I write also. The one who lives with me will know the truth, and it is truth you seek—not answers.

"Listen and learn and receive—that is your answer for today, little heart that beats. I am here. Find me and learn, for I will not fail you, and you will know the truth and the answers. It is written."

MESSAGE OF LOVE
More, more, more, and even more, wrote the wonderful person who loved it. *I want to write more and be more of a writer.*

Liking the hearing and the calling, she wrote more and went to bed later; later and later and later. And, later still, she wrote into the night. Wondering if this was to be her lifestyle, she asked the power to make her name famous once more—famous in its own likeness to her real name, which had lost its fame.

"Why try?" the power considered the request. "Why try to be who you are not when you are this name and not the other, which is nicer, I agree, but not you."

Wondering about this, the lady considered her reply to the one who asked, knowing that the one who asked already knew the answer.

"I cannot use my name, dear power that asks, for this book has truth that those who find it will not want; for they want measures of it in their lives, but also measures of lies. Lies that cannot hurt another, it is so, but lies that allow the wondering, beautiful human to accept their life as it is and not as it can be."

"Write this to that person who reads," answered the force of good in all lives who want it. "Say to this wonderful being: *You are mine to love and to care for. You are beautiful inside your soul, which has darkness wanting to envelope it. Say to the darkness: You may not, for I choose the light in this world and the next.* And then the human will know the truth: that I am it, and I care for those who love me back."

Written today is this asked-for tale, which is now on paper. Paper that sends a message of love to the reader who reads with an open mind—a mind that sees and hears and seeks and does not send viticulture's of hate by mail of any kind.

Remember me if you do; for this day, I hold my name secret. Do you? Give then to ways of love, and the lover who protects is also yours.

YOUR MISSION

Small, forthright changes were made to the book.

"Worthwhile," said the writer.

"Worthwhile," said the printer.

"Worthwhile," said the readers.

Worth the while of the changes—for additional hope is not ever without weakness, it's true, but it also has a cautionary tale to tell. And this is the tale: make the book large enough to include the additions, for here is the reader's choice: many will say, "Thank you," and some will say, "I understand." And it is those who understand who will prevail in their day—the day of action—for this world needs its leaders, and this writer needs your will to lead.

Be one who wins, and cries will be found not in your household but in the homes of ferrets and makers of distain.

Lead, and you will be held accountable; it's foretold. Lead with this wonderous book in your library, and you will be found upright and faithful to your cause.

Achievers are of all types and subtleties. Some may be large and some small, and some may be known and unknown. Some may make worlds of difference, and some just suburbs of hope and villages of water and fruit.

Change the world for the better, and you will live your life in the happiness foretold in the ways of this writer's hands, which have also worked to make you happier than you would have otherwise been.

Know this, and you know all truths; for now, this book is ended. There will be no other quite like it—just this one. Being at one with its teaching is to start a great, gyrated journey into the world of adults and better friends and wonderful gifts.

Frantic natures are not required; only peaceful ones with love to spare.

Fortitude will be yours to withstand assaults and be victorious. Trouble them not until the day they come—and come they will—for all are assaulted. You will not sink and will save your own victory for last—for the last are the first, and the first are the last.

Be at one with this understanding, and know this: you are loved—always.

Around the world, money has its ways, and around the world, police have theirs. And around the world, you will have yours: a friendship; a finding; a fun-filled aspect of light and living; a greeting at the asked-for time; a help when needed; a fine avoided; a writer alleviated.

Sincerely yours, a kindred spirit,

Review this book for other Seekers

Seekers, see your name with this hope added to it for others to find—whether you liked this book or not; for the ones who seek life are also helped by the ones who seek trust.

A byte is never enough. The hope of this world is in you, for all who are called are also filled with wonderful fretful ways that others enjoy. Believe this and know that your kindness is also necessary for others to see your good works.

Believe and call them with your wisdom, and write, if you care to, about this book. The length is not a calling; the work is not a requirement; the line is not a white coat. Lift the ones who are not whole to this worldly wisdom and make your hope for a better world better than it is now.

The writer makes this request: *"Seekers, please leave a review for the world to find the truth and the way. A wonderful day for all if you do—written and believed; a calling for those who seek. And a financial blessing for this charitable cause:* **Fleeing from war and entering a new dawn are many***.*

Help them, and you will also be helped; change will come, and so will blessings."

Charley Lane

charleylane.com

Coming Next

In the Tales for Serious Seekers of Truth series

Clarity Tales
for Really Serious Seekers of Truth

The book of all books is now here for all who seek to ask the power for love and to know it more clearly, for *Clarity* is the name of this edition: an edition with new clarity for the Seekers—clarity given from above.

Ask, and you will hear and see and know more than before; read, and you will kindly adhere—for in this day and this hour, the kindly who adhere will be blessed by the power who writes.

Time therefore to begin...